GIFTED
HERE TODAY,
GONE TOMORROW

Also available:

Gifted: Out of Sight, Out of Mind

Gifted: Better Late Than Never

Look out for:

Gifted: Finders Keepers

GIFTED
HERE TODAY,
GONE TOMORROW

MARILYN KAYE

KINGFISHER
NEW YORK

KINGFISHER
LONDON & NEW YORK

Copyright © 2009 by Marilyn Kaye
Published in the United States by Kingfisher,
175 Fifth Ave., New York, NY 10010
Kingfisher is an imprint of Macmillan Children's Books, London.

Distributed in the U.S. by Macmillan, 175 Fifth Ave., New York, NY 10010
Distributed in Canada by H.B. Fenn and Company Ltd., 34 Nixon Road,
Bolton, Ontario L7E 1W2

Library of Congress Cataloging-in-Publication data has been applied for.

ISBN: 978-0-7534-6310-9

Kingfisher books are available for special promotions and premiums.
For details contact: Special Markets Department, Macmillan,
175 Fifth Avenue, New York, NY 10010.

For more information, please visit www.kingfisherpublications.com

Typeset by Intype Libra Limited
Printed and bound in the UK by CPI Mackays, Chatham ME5 8TD
1 3 5 7 9 8 6 4 2

For my goddaughter, Iris,
her brother Octave, and their parents,
Muriel Berthelot and Jean-François Marti

Chapter One

SOMETIMES EMILY WASN'T sure if she was dreaming or having one of her visions. Usually it happened in the early morning, just before her alarm went off.

On this particular Monday morning, she was pretty sure she was awake. She knew her eyes were open because she could see her chest of drawers, her desk, and her bookcase, with her old collection of dolls from many lands lining the top shelf. Dim sunlight was coming through the muslin curtains on her window, and she could even see the sweater she'd left hanging on the bedpost the day before.

But at the same time, she saw something else, something that didn't belong in her bedroom—an image, sort of translucent, that floated before her eyes. Even though it wasn't very distinct, she recognized the image immediately—it was one of her classes at school, her so-called gifted class.

There was the teacher, Madame, sitting at her desk. In their usual seats sat her classmates: Ken, Amanda, Tracey, Martin, and the others. She could even see herself . . . but wait, there were only eight students—someone wasn't there.

It was funny, in a way: they all complained about the class—some of the students even hated it—but they rarely missed it. And with only nine students in the class, no one could skip it without being noticed. But who was missing in her vision? Jenna was there; she could see Sarah; and there was Charles in his wheelchair . . .

Carter was missing. It made sense that she hadn't realized this immediately. Since Carter didn't speak, he didn't call attention to himself, and it was easy to forget he was even in the room. But normally, he *was* there, physically at least, so this was odd.

Then her alarm clock rang, and the classroom disappeared. She sat up, reached out to her nightstand and turned it off. The image was gone, and she still wasn't absolutely sure if it had been a dream or a vision. She'd dreamed about her class before, but the dreams had been like most of the dreams she had, full of silly things, like Ken swinging from a light fixture or Charles dancing on Madame's desk. The image she'd just experienced had seemed so real . . . yes, it must have been a vision.

It probably wasn't a big deal though. Carter might act like a zombie, but he was a human being and just as susceptible to getting the flu or an upset stomach as anyone else.

"Emily! Are you up?"

Her mother's voice sounded testy, as if this was the second or third time she'd called to Emily—which was entirely possible. Emily's visions, even the trivial ones, always seemed to require all her senses, so she might not have heard her mother's earlier calls. Or maybe she'd really been sleeping. It was so hard to tell . . .

"I'm up," she called back. Dragging herself out of bed, she left her room and went across the hall to the bathroom. While brushing her teeth, she caught a glimpse of her reflection in the mirror and almost choked on the toothpaste. Why was her face so blurry? Was this the beginning of another vision?

No, it was just that she hadn't put her contacts in yet. Having done that, she went back to her bedroom where she spent about twenty seconds selecting her clothes. This activity never took very long since she essentially wore the same thing every day, with some minor variations in her choice of T-shirt or sweater. She didn't bother with makeup. Until very recently, she'd worn glasses, and what was the point of makeup when your glasses covered half your face? And even though she had contacts now and her face was more visible, she hadn't yet bought any cosmetics. Makeup required concentration, and the way Emily daydreamed, she knew she'd end up putting lipstick on her eyelids.

So when she checked herself out in the mirror, she didn't encounter anything surprising. In fact, having examined photos of herself as a small child, she knew she'd looked pretty much the same all her life. In her class picture from first grade, she could see the same oval face, long, straight nose, and full lips she saw now. She was still wearing her long, straight brown hair in the same style, which was actually no style at all.

She wondered if she would still look like this when she was an adult. But as usual, when she really wanted to see the future, she couldn't.

"Emily! You're going to be late!"

"I'm coming!" She grabbed the sweater hanging on the bedpost and ran down the hall to the kitchen. Her mother had set out a choice of cereals on the small kitchen table, and Emily helped herself.

"Did you sleep well?" her mother asked. She asked Emily the same question every day, and usually Emily responded with an automatic "yes." But this time, thinking about her confusion that morning, she looked at her mother thoughtfully.

"Mom . . . do you ever think you're awake but you're really sleeping? Or the other way around?"

Her mother looked at her sharply. "Are you having those visions again?"

I never stopped, Emily wanted to reply, but she knew this would only upset her mother. She never liked talking about Emily's gift, but every now and then, Emily took a chance and brought up the subject. She couldn't help hoping that there would come a time when her mother would want to listen to her. But the expression on her mother's face told her that now was not the time, so she didn't even bother to respond to her mother's question.

"Is there any orange juice?" she asked instead.

Her mother was clearly relieved to have the change in subject. "Of course, it's in the refrigerator. There's grape juice, too—it was on sale at the grocery store."

Her mother was always on the lookout for items on sale. She had a good job as the office manager for a company, but since the death of Emily's father, she was the only one in the house who earned money.

A couple of other kids at Emily's school had also lost a parent, and although she'd never talked to them about it, she assumed they suffered the same kind of sadness she did. But she couldn't imagine that either of them felt as guilty about it.

"By the way, I'll be late getting home today," her mother told her. "I've got an appointment with Tony."

There was nothing unusual about that. Her mother wore her hair in a short, layered style, and every six weeks she went to see Tony at Budget Scissors for a cut. But out of nowhere, Emily had a sudden vision, and she was alarmed.

"I don't think you should do that, Mom. Not today."

"Why not?"

The vision was shockingly clear. Her mother's normally soft curls were a frizzy, snarled mess. "I can see you. After your appointment. Maybe Tony's in a bad mood or something—I don't know—but he's not going to give you a nice haircut today."

Emily watched the bewilderment on her mother's face turn to irritation, and she didn't have to be a fortuneteller to know the annoyance wasn't directed at Tony the hairdresser.

"Emily, stop it, right this minute! You're talking utter nonsense."

There was no point in arguing with her, but Emily had to make one point. "Mom, if my visions are nonsense, why do you think they put me in the class for people with special gifts?"

Her mother's lips tightened. "I don't want to discuss this now, Emily. We're leaving in two minutes."

She left the kitchen. Emily finished her cereal and went to search for her school stuff. She wasn't angry at her mother for not understanding her gift. How could she be angry when Emily didn't understand it herself? Passing through the living room, she paused to look at the framed photograph on the wall. It was something she did whenever she thought about her so-called gift, but it never provided any answers. Only more questions.

The photo was only eight years old, but her mother looked a lot younger in it. Maybe it was because she was smiling, not just with her lips but with her eyes—an expression Emily didn't see on her face very often. She had one hand on the shoulder of five-year-old Emily. And on Emily's other side was her father.

From the angle of the photo, it seemed that no matter where Emily stood when she looked at it, his eyes were on her. And sometimes she felt that he was looking at her with disappointment, like he was reminding her that she could have saved his life.

There were times when she wished she couldn't recall the memory so easily. Was it her very first vision? She couldn't be sure, but it was the first one that had a real effect on her life. And it had happened at such an ordinary moment.

It was as detailed a memory as if it had occurred the day before. Her mother was brushing Emily's hair, getting her ready for a day at kindergarten. Her father was putting some papers in his briefcase.

The image had come to her out of nowhere, just like the vision she'd had of her class that morning. She could see her father walking out the front door, heading to the car he'd parked across the street. She could see him stepping off the curb without looking both ways. Another car, moving very fast, came screaming around the corner. And hit him.

She wanted to tell him about this frightening vision, but he was already heading to the door. She knew all she had to say was something like, "Wait, Daddy, I have something to tell you," but she didn't. Even today, she still didn't know why she hadn't spoken up. Was she afraid he'd laugh at her?

The "why" didn't really matter now. Her father was killed by a speeding car and it happened just the way she'd seen it in her vision. And maybe, just maybe, if she *had* told him about her vision, he would have been more careful crossing the street. If he had stopped to listen to her, maybe the speeding car would have gone down her street before he even went outside. At least her mother couldn't blame her for her father's death, since she didn't really believe Emily could see into the future. But Emily could blame herself.

Now, whenever she had serious visions that could affect someone's life, she told that person. But they didn't always appreciate it, and usually they didn't believe her. Which was understandable . . . because sometimes the visions were wrong. Well, maybe not completely wrong, but not exactly . . . clear. Like the time she told Terri Boyd in her English class that she was going to fall off the balance beam in her gymnastics competition that day. Only Terri didn't fall—not then. But at her competition the following weekend, she tumbled off. And Terri actually blamed Emily for it, telling her *she* put the idea in her head!

"Ready?" her mother asked.

Emily picked up her backpack and followed her mother outside. But just as her mother was locking the door, she had another vision. It was funny how this could happen. She could go for days without a vision and then have a dozen in one morning.

"Mom, I forgot something. I'll be right back." Ignoring her mother's protests, she ran back inside and down the hall to her room. She found what she needed in her bookcase, stuck it in her backpack, and hurried back to join her mother.

"What did you forget?" her mother wanted to know.

"A book I have to lend Jenna," Emily replied. Which was the truth—she just didn't tell her how she knew Jenna would need the book.

The five-minute drive to Meadowbrook Middle School was free of visions, but the image of the gifted class without Carter was still in her head. When she arrived at school, she considered looking for Madame to tell her about it, but Madame was always warning her not to speak up too quickly. She'd told Emily to think about her visions, to examine them and consider them before jumping to conclusions. Emily wasn't so sure about that—she saw what she saw, and that wouldn't change just because she thought about it. But Madame seemed to think otherwise, so she decided to wait until the gifted class met. Maybe she would have a clearer vision by then.

She was still vision-free at lunchtime, when she set her tray down on the cafeteria table next to Tracey and across from Jenna. Jenna was in the process of trying to get Tracey to use *her* special gift on Jenna's behalf.

"Ms. Stanford always does her photocopying during fourth period, and you've got study period then, so you won't miss a class. Just get yourself into the teachers' lounge and look at the test while she's copying it. You don't have to memorize the whole thing—I just need to know what the essay question is going to be."

Clearly this discussion had been going on for some time. Wearily, Tracey shook her head. "That's cheating, Jenna. I can't help you."

"Of course you *can*," Jenna insisted, narrowing her kohl-rimmed eyes. "You just *won't*."

"Actually, it's both," Tracey said. "I can't always go invisible on demand."

"You're getting a lot better at it though," Emily pointed out.

"Yeah, but it's not easy. Remember why I started disappearing? It was because no one paid any attention to me. If I tried talking to people, they didn't hear me. I'd raise my hand in class and the teacher wouldn't see me. Even my own parents ignored me. I *felt* invisible, so I became invisible."

Jenna gazed at her quizzically. "But you don't feel invisible anymore, do you? How come you can still disappear?"

"I have to try and remember how it was back then, when I felt like nobody. That can be pretty depressing, so I don't like doing it. But if I'm feeling too confident or strong or really good about myself, it's *really* hard."

For Emily, it was comforting to hear that others couldn't always rely on their gifts. Tracey couldn't disappear just by snapping her fingers. And Jenna, who could read minds, couldn't read *everyone's* mind. With some people, she had no problem—their minds were an open book. But she couldn't read her own mother's mind, nor Madame's, nor Carter's.

And with the other gifted students, she complained about how sometimes she could read them and sometimes she couldn't. Of course, her classmates would recommend that she shouldn't even try, but Jenna, being Jenna, didn't take advice well.

"I'm sorry, Jenna," Tracey continued. "I know you think I'm being a prig, but cheating is wrong. Why can't you just study for the test like everyone else?"

Jenna made a face. "What's the point of learning everything when you only really need to learn what you're going to be tested on?" Then she brightened. "Hey, I just had a brilliant idea. I could ask Ms. Stanford some questions about the test. Then she'll start thinking about it, and I'll read her mind!"

Emily thought that was a pretty good idea, but Tracey disapproved. "It's not right, Jenna. It's still cheating."

Jenna shrugged. "It's the teachers' fault. I wouldn't have to cheat if they didn't give us so much work. I've got an essay due on Thursday, the test tomorrow, a book report to give today—" she stopped suddenly, and snatched up her backpack. Frantically, she began to search the contents.

"What's the book?" Tracey asked.

"*The Diary of Anne Frank*. And I left it at home." She dropped the backpack and looked at the others mournfully. "Can you believe it? I actually read the whole book, I wrote the report, and I marked passages to read out loud. And now I don't have the book."

Emily reached into *her* backpack. "Surprise," she said, handing over her own copy of the book.

Jenna grabbed it out of her hands. "Wow! Thanks, Em."

"How did you know she'd need it?" Tracey asked Emily.

"Jenna told me she was reading it last weekend. Remember, Jenna? You said it made you cry."

"It made me *sad*," Jenna contradicted her. "I didn't *cry*."

Tracey shook her head impatiently. "No, how did you know she would forget to bring her copy to school?"

"I had a vision," Emily said proudly.

"Cool!" Tracey exclaimed. "You had an accurate premonition."

Jenna disagreed. "But you can't say for sure that you were predicting the future."

"Why not?" Emily asked.

"Because you know how I'm always forgetting stuff, and you knew I was giving this report today. So you brought me your copy of *Anne Frank* in case I left mine at home. Which was nice of you, and I appreciate it. But you didn't know for sure that I'd forget the book."

"But I *did* know," Emily insisted. "I saw it."

Tracey backed her up. "Emily's been getting better and better at making predictions, Jenna."

Jenna looked at Emily. "Hey, I'm not saying you don't have a gift. You just don't know how to use it very well."

It was typical of Jenna to speak like that—frankly, without always thinking about other people's feelings. Emily tried not to take it personally, but she couldn't help it.

"So you think my gift is worthless."

Tracey was much kinder. "She didn't mean that, Emily. Okay, maybe you don't have much control over your gift right now, but you're definitely

16

improving." She glared at Jenna, demanding a confirmation.

"Yeah, I guess you're getting a little better," Jenna acknowledged.

It wasn't much of a compliment, and it didn't make Emily feel any happier. She was glad to hear Tracey change the subject.

"How are things at home?" she asked Jenna.

Jenna produced her usual nonchalant shrug, but she punctuated it with a grin and said, "Not bad." Given her resistance to sounding overly positive or optimistic, "not bad" could easily mean "excellent." Emily remembered that Jenna had stayed with Tracey's family for two weeks while her mother was in the hospital, but her mother was home now, and Jenna was back there with her. Emily ventured a question.

"And your mother, she's . . ." she hesitated, unsure of how to put this delicately. Pretty much everyone knew that Jenna's mother had been in rehab. "She's doing okay?"

Jenna rephrased this in her own blunt way. "You mean, is she sober? Yeah, so far."

"I bet she's going to make it this time," Tracey declared.

"Maybe," Jenna allowed. She shot a look at Emily. "Don't you even *think* about making any predictions."

"I have no intention of even trying," Emily assured her. She knew Jenna didn't mean to insult her, but Emily couldn't help feeling a twinge of irritation. She got up before her feelings could show on her face. "I'm going to get some water."

Beside the water fountain was a row of trash cans where students emptied their trays. Emily saw Sarah Miller, another of her classmates, poking around the contents of one of them.

"What are you doing?" Emily asked her.

Sarah looked up. Her heart-shaped face was utterly woebegone.

"I lost my ring," she wailed.

Emily winced. Being someone who often lost or misplaced things, she could totally empathize.

"Did you take it off?"

"I don't think so. I leave it on all the time, even when I wash my hands. It must have fallen off, but I don't know where or when. I just noticed that it wasn't on my finger." She touched the ring finger on her right hand as she spoke. Emily stared at it. If she concentrated very hard, she might get a vision. Sometimes this worked, sometimes it didn't.

She was in luck—her vision began to blur and her eyes glazed over. An image began to emerge . . . "You'll find it."

Since Sarah was in the gifted class, too, she knew about Emily's ability, but unlike Jenna, she actually had some respect for it. Her eyes lit up. "Really? Where?"

"It's in your coat pocket."

Sarah's brow furrowed. "You know, that's possible. I wore a coat today, and I forgot my gloves so I kept my hands in the pockets. It could have come off there."

Emily nodded. "It was a pretty clear vision. It was in the bottom of a coat pocket."

Sarah was getting excited. "So I could find it now if I go and look."

Emily hesitated. This was the weakest area of her gift—the question of "when." She might see an event, like Terri Boyd falling off the balance beam, but she might not be sure when it would happen. But in this particular case . . .

"If that's where it fell off, it must be there now," she said decisively.

Sarah looked at the clock on the wall. "The coat's in my locker. If I hurry, I have time to look before class. Thanks, Emily!"

Emily beamed as she watched Sarah run out of the cafeteria. But her smile faded as she noticed the girls at a nearby table staring at her. She really had to learn to think before she spoke. Britney Teller and Sophie Greene were gaping at her, with open mouths and wide eyes. Amanda Beeson, Emily's gifted classmate, was with them, but her expression was very different. She was glaring at Emily, with "urge to kill" written all over her face.

Britney spoke first. "Emily, can you *see* things? Like a psychic?"

Emily didn't have to respond—Amanda took care of that for her.

"Yeah, sure, Emily's a gypsy fortuneteller," she declared. "Show us your crystal ball, Emily." And just in case anyone didn't hear the sarcasm in her voice, she started giggling in an especially mean way, something she could do very well, in keeping with her reputation as one of Meadowbrook's top mean girls.

Immediately Britney and Sophie joined in, doing their best imitation of Amanda's laugh. Emily could feel her own face redden. She had about as much control of her complexion as she had over her predictions.

She made her way back to her own table, where Jenna and Tracey gazed at her sympathetically. Obviously they'd heard everything.

"In all fairness," Tracey said, "Amanda did the right thing, covering for you like that."

"I know," Emily replied glumly. "But did she have to do it so *loudly*?"

"You can't really blame her," Jenna said. "*We* know she's not really that nasty, but she has to work at maintaining her reputation if she wants to keep her status with those kids she hangs out with."

This was all true, but Emily was still feeling embarrassed. She looked forward to the gifted class, where Sarah's gratitude might cheer her up.

But when she entered room 209, she could see at a glance that Sarah wasn't any happier than she'd been when Emily first saw her in the cafeteria. Her disconsolate classmate had her elbows on her desk and her chin in her hands, and there was no ring on her finger.

She looked up as Emily approached. "I checked all my pockets. It wasn't there." Her tone wasn't accusing—Sarah was too nice for that—but Emily tried to defend herself.

"Maybe it's in the pocket of another coat," she offered, but without much conviction.

Sarah shook her head. "I haven't worn any other coat recently."

"I'm sorry," Emily said.

Sarah gave her a sad smile, as if to assure her she didn't blame Emily, but Emily felt guilty anyway. She took her seat and mentally checked her score for the day. She'd known that Jenna would forget her book (even though Jenna refused to consider it a prediction), so she gave herself a point for that. But Sarah's missing ring put her back at zero. What other premonitions had she had? There was her mother's hair, but she wouldn't know the answer to that one till she got home.

She'd predicted something else . . . Of course! Carter Street. According to her vision, he shouldn't be in class today. It was almost time for the bell, and she surveyed the room. Martin, Jenna, and Amanda were in their seats . . . Charles rolled in, followed by Tracey, and at the last minute, Ken hurried into the room.

The bell went off. As it rang, Madame entered and closed the door. Emily felt a rush of satisfaction—Carter was missing!

Madame went to her desk and looked over the room. "Where's Carter? Has anyone seen him?"

Nobody had. Madame's brow furrowed. "I can't remember Carter ever missing a class." She looked at a piece of paper on her desk. "He's not on the approved absentee list."

"Maybe he's cutting class," Martin ventured.

Madame wouldn't even consider that, and Emily understood why. Carter was like a robot—he did what he was supposed to do and what he was told to do. Nothing more, nothing less. He didn't speak, his face showed no expressions, and according to Jenna, he had no thoughts—yet somehow he functioned, physically at least, like a regular person.

No one knew who he really was or where he came from—he'd been found a year earlier on Carter Street, and that was the name he'd been given. So far, he hadn't exhibited any particular gift, and Emily didn't know why he was in their gifted class. Maybe it was because he was just different, like the rest of them.

She could tell that Madame was concerned, and her initial joy at being correct in her premonition evaporated. Carter's absence wasn't a good thing, and Emily was ashamed for taking pleasure from it.

It was warm in the classroom, and Madame started to take off her suit jacket.

"Oh, I almost forgot." She put a hand in her pocket. "Does this belong to anyone?"

"My ring!" Sarah cried out. She went to the desk to take it. "Oh, thank you, Madame. Where did you find it?"

"On the floor," the teacher replied. "It must have slipped off your finger and rolled away. You might want to have it made smaller so it won't be loose, Sarah."

"I will," Sarah said, and returned to her desk. She didn't look at Emily as she passed her, but Emily sank down in her seat anyway. So the ring had been found—she'd been right about that. But not in Sarah's pocket.

But wait . . . what had she envisioned, exactly? Had she actually seen *Sarah* put her hand in her pocket? All she'd seen in the vision was the ring in a pocket. And that was where it had been. It just wasn't in the pocket she'd assumed it would be in. So in a way, she'd been right. She just hadn't understood her own premonition.

But that didn't make her feel much better. She had visions—so what? She didn't know what they meant. What was the good of having a gift if you couldn't even understand it?

She didn't have any more visions at school that day, and her mood didn't improve. This wasn't helped by the fact that she went home with an unusually large amount of homework.

At least the homework required all her attention,

and she didn't think about her mother and her hair appointment. But when she heard the door open and her mother's call of "I'm home," the memory of her premonition came back. She hurried out to the living room.

Her mother was just taking off her coat. "Hi, honey. How was your day?"

When Emily didn't respond right away, her mother repeated her question. "Em? Did you have a nice day?"

"Oh, yeah, it was okay. Sorry, I was looking at your hair."

Her mother patted the nicely trimmed soft curls. "Do you like it?"

Emily nodded. "Tony did a nice job."

"Actually, Tony was called away on a family emergency, so I had Lauren this time. What shall we do about dinner?" She breezed past Emily and went into the kitchen.

Emily couldn't think about dinner—she was too busy pondering the implications of another messed-up premonition. Was it just because Tony hadn't been there and another hairdresser had done the job?

Would her mother's next appointment with Tony be a disaster? Or was it just a false prediction?

It was all too depressing. This talent she had—it could be so precious, so valuable. So many people would love to have her gift, and they could do wonderful things with it.

But in her own clumsy hands—no, in her own clumsy brain—it was worthless.

Chapter Two

EMILY COULD FEEL HER mother's worried eyes on her as they sat across from each other at the table.

"Emily? Are you feeling all right? You're not eating."

She was right. And on the plate in front of her was one of her absolute favorites—macaroni and cheese.

"I'm not very hungry," she replied, but she stuck her fork into the cheesy pasta anyway.

Her mother still looked concerned. She really cared, Emily knew that, and for a mother, she was usually pretty understanding. About most things, at least.

"Mom," Emily began, and then she lost her nerve. Her mother sighed.

"You *are* having those visions again, aren't you." It

was a statement, not a question, but Emily answered anyway. She wanted so desperately to talk about it.

"Sort of."

"Do you talk about this in your . . . your class? Isn't your teacher supposed to help you . . . *deal* with your problem?"

That was how her mother saw her gift—as a problem. When Emily was asked to join the class, Madame had told her mother that its purpose was to help the students channel and control their talents. But somehow her mother had convinced herself that the purpose of it was to help the students get rid of their delusions.

"We talk about our *gifts*," Emily said, emphasizing the last word. "We talk about how to develop them and make the most of them."

As usual, her mother didn't hear her. "Em, honey . . . if you're not getting any help from that Madame person, maybe you should go back to see Dr. Mackle."

Emily shuddered. Her mother had dragged her to the psychologist two years ago. He'd treated her like a six-year-old with an imaginary friend and said her visions were simply the product of an overactive, creative imagination. No, Dr. Mackle couldn't help her.

She gave up. "I'm fine, Mom. I've just got a lot of homework and I'm a little stressed out."

That was something her mother could understand. "Well, you go ahead and get to work," she said briskly. "I'll take care of the dishes."

"I'll clear the table," Emily offered. While she was collecting the dishes, the phone rang. Her mother got to it first.

"Hello? Hi, Tracey. Yes, she's here, but she's got a lot of homework so don't talk too long. Oh really? Okay, here she is." She handed the cordless phone to Emily. "Tracey's having some problems with the homework and she wants to talk to you about it."

This couldn't be true—Madame hadn't given them any homework, and she and Tracey didn't have any other classes together. Emily took the phone and played along.

"Hi, I'm taking the phone to my room so I can

look at the assignment." That was for her mother's benefit. Once in her own room, she closed the door and fell down on her bed with the phone.

"Hi, what's up?"

"Not much. Wait a sec, I gotta yell at the clones. Hey, you guys, out of my room! Now!"

Emily could picture Tracey's identical little sisters, the infamous Devon Seven, surrounding her and begging for stories. As an only child, Emily used to envy Tracey. But after spending some time in Tracey's house, she now understood one of the reasons why Tracey was so intent on learning to disappear at will—so she could really and truly hide from them sometimes.

"Hi, I'm back. I just called to find out how you're doing. You seemed really down today."

Emily wasn't surprised that Tracey had been so aware of her feelings. Tracey was practically an authority on being depressed, having spent around five years in that condition.

"I'm confused," Emily confessed. "My visions are so—so *messy*. Sometimes I wonder if I really have a gift at all."

"Of course you do," Tracey assured her. "Think of all the times you've told me what's going to happen! Remember when you asked me if I'd ever had measles?"

Emily recalled the strange premonition she'd had a few months earlier. She kept envisioning Tracey and thinking "measles." "Yeah, I remember."

"Well, why did you ask me that? Because you knew the clones were going to come down with measles and you were worried that I might catch it."

"But why didn't I just see your sisters with measles in my vision? It's like, every time I get a premonition, it's not clear—it's all twisted and mixed-up."

"Maybe because the future is never all that clear. I mean, it can always change, can't it?"

"I guess," Emily replied, but she wasn't so sure about that. If the future could change, then how could she see it before it happened? Like today . . . "I had a vision this morning that Carter wouldn't be in class today."

"*That* must have been a clear vision," Tracey said. "And it was accurate."

There was a rap on her door. "Em, don't stay on the phone too long. You've got homework."

"I gotta go," Emily told Tracey. "Thanks for calling."

"Want to make a quick prediction before we hang up?" Tracey asked.

"I can try," Emily said. "Ask me a question."

"Um . . . Will Carter be back in class tomorrow?"

Emily half-closed her eyes, so that her eyesight was blurred, and waited to see if any kind of image formed. She was pleased when a vision of the class began to form.

"No . . . he won't be there. Wait—someone else is missing, too."

"Who?"

Emily looked over the faces in the fuzzy image. "It's you! Are you feeling okay? Maybe you're going to be sick."

"I feel fine," Tracey assured her. "Maybe I'll be invisible."

"Are you going to try to disappear tomorrow?"

"I don't know. Maybe. I practice every day, but usually at home in my room."

"Well, don't do it just so I'll think my prediction was accurate."

Tracey laughed. "See you tomorrow."

When she saw Tracey at their usual table in the cafeteria the next day, she wasn't sure if she was relieved or disappointed. Of course she was glad Tracey wasn't sick, and that she hadn't done a disappearing act just to make Emily feel better about herself (although that was the kind of thing Tracey would do). But her presence was more evidence that Emily's predictions were half-baked at best.

Still, she forced a smile as she carried her lunch to the table. "I'm glad to see you," she assured Tracey.

Tracey sighed. "I'm sorry."

"Sorry about what?" Jenna appeared at the table, carrying a lunch tray.

"Oh, nothing," Tracey said quickly. "Hey, you bought your lunch!"

Emily had noticed that, too. Jenna always brought a sandwich from home. With her mother's problems, the family had lived on public assistance, and Jenna was always short of cash.

Jenna set the tray on the table. "Yeah, how about that? My mother got a job!"

"Wow, that's great!" Tracey exclaimed.

"Doing what?" Emily asked.

"She's going to be a secretary at the hospital! That's what she used to be, a secretary, and while she was in rehab, she told one of the nurses. And it turned out she remembers all her computer skills." She turned to Emily. "Guess you didn't see that coming, did you?"

Emily's smile faded. "No. I haven't been having many successful premonitions lately."

"Hey, it's okay," Jenna said, taking her seat. "I wouldn't have believed you if you'd predicted it." She looked beyond them and grimaced. "Oh damn. What do *they* want?"

Emily turned to see three of Amanda's friends sauntering toward them. They were whispering and smirking, and she steeled herself for an insult.

Nina, the nastiest one, spoke. "Emily, I'm trying out for cheerleading today. Could you tell me if I'm going to make the squad?"

Emily sighed. "No."

"No, you can't tell me, or no, I'm not going to make the squad?"

Britney and Sophie started giggling furiously.

Emily considered a snappy retort, something like "I won't waste my gift on something stupid like cheerleading," but of course she couldn't let them know she really could see into the future.

Tracey saved her. "She doesn't know and she doesn't care, so leave her alone."

Nina faked a look of wide-eyed innocence. "But I thought Emily could tell the future."

Jenna rolled her eyes. "Oh, *please*. Emily doesn't even know what day it will be tomorrow."

To her horror, Emily felt her eyes well up. She knew Jenna was just trying to convince the girls it was all a joke, that the idea of Emily being able to predict the future was ridiculous. But in a way, what Jenna said was almost true, and that was what hurt. She managed to keep her expression frozen until the girls walked away, and then a tear escaped.

Tracey saw it. "Oh, Emily, you can't care what those girls think."

"I don't," Emily said fiercely, staring at Jenna.

"Hey, I was just trying to help out," Jenna protested.

"I know," Tracey said. "But Emily's feeling pretty sensitive about her gift these days."

Jenna's expression changed. "Really? Hey, I'm sorry, Em. I was just fooling around."

"It's okay," Emily sighed. "I just feel like my gift is awfully weak. I mean, compared with the others in our class."

"What about Carter?" Jenna said. "He doesn't even have a gift. At least, he's never shown us one."

"Speaking of Carter, Emily knew he wouldn't be in class yesterday," Tracey told her. "She was right about that." She turned to Emily. "And you said he won't be there today, right? I'll bet you're right again."

"But even if I am, I thought you wouldn't be there either. So I'd only be half right."

"Have you talked to Madame about this?" Jenna wanted to know.

Tracey was taken aback. "Since when do you trust teachers?"

"I don't," Jenna said quickly. "Not regular

teachers. But Madame's . . . okay. I think she's different. She understands stuff."

Tracey looked thoughtful. "Do you really think she understands our gifts?"

Jenna shrugged. "Well, she knows about them and she doesn't treat us like freaks. That's enough for me."

It was enough for Emily, too. At least Madame would be willing to listen. She pushed her barely touched tray away.

"Maybe you're right. I'm going to go see if I can talk to her now."

She was in luck—Madame was already in the classroom, going through some papers at her desk. Emily stood in the doorway and coughed loudly. The teacher looked up. She didn't smile, but she spoke kindly.

"Yes, Emily?"

Emily hesitated. Madame looked preoccupied, like she had something on her mind. Maybe this wasn't a good time. But then Madame spoke again.

"Have you had a vision?"

"I'm always having visions," Emily said. "That's the problem. Because they're not always right.

No, that's not exactly true. They're just not completely right."

"We've talked about this before," Madame reminded her. "Are you examining the visions? Are you looking for clues that could help you make sense of them, to make the most of your visions?"

Madame was right—Emily had heard all this before. But she still didn't get it. She reported the visions as she saw them—what else could she do?

"Can you give me an example?" she asked the teacher.

Madame didn't get the opportunity. Another teacher appeared at the classroom door and spoke in a rush.

"Could you come with me? It's Martin Cooper . . ."

"Of course." Madame rose quickly. "I'm sorry, Emily, I have to go."

Emily didn't need any explanation for her need to leave—she could guess what was happening in some other classroom. Skinny little Martin Cooper had a gift that only served himself. If he was teased or ridiculed—which happened frequently, since he was such a whiny, babyish nerd—he went more than a little nuts. His scrawny body was suddenly endowed with an almost superhuman strength, and he became violent. Madame was the only one who could calm him down.

Yes, like Jenna said, Madame understood the special students. Unlike most of their parents, she accepted the reality of the gifts and she believed in her students' abilities. But unfortunately for Emily, the other students' gifts usually took up more of Madame's time.

Ken could be tormented by the voices of the deceased, and he didn't seem to have much control over them. Emily often wondered how Ken had developed such a weird gift. He never really said much about it except to complain when dead people kept trying to talk to him. He certainly wasn't happy about it, ever, and Madame always seemed to have a special sympathy for him.

Charles, like Martin, had a gift which could create big problems that demanded Madame's immediate attention. He couldn't make his legs move—he'd been paralyzed since birth—and somehow he'd developed telekinesis, being able to make things move with his mind. And if he was in a bad mood, which was pretty often, he used his gift in very destructive ways.

Amanda could take over other people's bodies. If she felt very sorry for a person, she could end up *being* that person. Tracey, who'd been occupied by Amanda for a couple of weeks, said this was why Amanda was so nasty to some people—she couldn't risk caring about them.

On the other hand, Sarah didn't demand much attention from Madame, which was interesting, since she had the greatest power of all—she could make people do whatever she wanted them to do. At least, that's what they'd all been told. It was hard to believe, since Sarah was usually so nice and easygoing. And they'd never seen any evidence of her gift, since Sarah refused to use it. That was why Madame didn't have to watch her so closely. Still, the power was there, so Madame had to find Sarah pretty intriguing.

And what could Emily do? Offer predictions that might or might not come true. Not exactly something that would make Madame jump out of her seat.

There was still some time before the bell, and Emily could have gone back to the cafeteria and rejoined her friends, but she had nothing to tell them, so what was the point? She went to her seat, sat down, and half-closed her eyes.

Show me something, she told her mind. She waited for a vision. It took a while, but finally an image began to form. To her disappointment, the image turned out to be Amanda's friend Nina. She was jumping around in front of some uniformed cheerleaders. Then she performed a cartwheel, a split, and a back handspring. Something went wrong with the last move, and she ended up flat on her butt.

So Nina wouldn't make the cheerleading squad. That was comforting but not very important. And nobody would care except Nina.

Jenna sauntered into the room and sat next to Emily. "What did Madame say?"

"Not much," Emily told her. "She got called out on a Martin emergency."

"Oh, too bad. Maybe you can talk to her after class."

And tell her what? Emily wondered dismally. That Amanda's friend Nina wouldn't make the cheerleading squad? Madame would care about that just about as much as Emily cared.

"Where's Tracey?" she asked, just to change the subject.

"She had to stop at her locker. Look, here comes Madame with Martin."

The teacher walked into the room with a hand firmly attached to Martin's shoulder. He was pouting, like a five-year-old who'd been caught with his hand in the cookie jar, and he took his seat without a word. One by one the other students came in, and the bell rang.

Madame surveyed the room. "I see Carter's still absent. Has anyone seen him?" No one had, and Madame frowned as she made a note on a paper. Then she looked up and asked the same question Emily had asked Jenna.

"Where's Tracey?"

"She went to her locker," Jenna offered, and Madame frowned again. She hated for students to be late.

But Tracey wasn't late for class. She didn't show up at all. And by the end of the hour, Emily could only think of one reason why.

Tracey meant well. She wanted Emily to cheer up, to feel confident about herself and her gift. She'd managed to make herself go invisible so Emily would believe that this particular prediction had come true. Maybe right this minute Tracey was sitting in that empty seat and hoping Emily was happy.

She looked at Tracey's usual desk, and for a second, she actually thought she could see her friend. It was all in her imagination, of course. But just in case Tracey was there, Emily offered a weak smile at the empty seat.

The bell rang. Jenna came to her side and looked at the empty seat. "She's getting pretty good at disappearing," she commented.

Before Emily could respond, Amanda paused on

her way out and spoke to her. "Why are you staring at Tracey's desk with that goofy smile?"

Jenna answered for her. "Emily predicted that Tracey wouldn't be in class today."

Amanda shrugged. "Nah, she's just being invisible."

"How can you be so sure about that?" Emily asked.

"Because it's more likely than one of your visions coming true."

Jenna, who would do or say anything to contradict Amanda, responded. "It's not just Tracey. Emily predicted that Carter wouldn't be in class yesterday."

"Big deal. So she actually got two predictions right." Amanda turned to Emily. "So tell me, Miss Know-It-All, who else is going to disappear tomorrow? Me, I hope. I hate this class."

Emily knew she was being mocked, but even so, she let her eyes glaze over to see if anything would be revealed. And she had a vision.

"Martin."

"Yeah, whatever," Amanda said airily and left the room.

Jenna didn't say anything, but her skeptical

45

expression told Emily she didn't have a whole lot more faith in Emily's prediction than Amanda had. So the next day, at least two people were pretty surprised when Martin didn't appear in class.

CHAPTER THREE

AS MADAME CLOSED THE door and Martin still hadn't appeared, Jenna turned around and gave Emily an appreciative nod. Emily didn't seem to notice—she had a dazed expression on her face. Which wasn't that unusual— she always looked a little dreamy and out of it.

Jenna hadn't meant to hurt Emily's feelings about her gift. She liked Emily. She might be a space cadet who cried a little too easily, but she was a good person, and she was a friend. And Jenna didn't have all that many friends.

That was pretty much her own fault—she knew that. She'd come to Meadowbrook Middle School after a brief stay in a program for troublemakers, and she hadn't kept that a secret. In fact, she'd acted like she was proud of her bad reputation and kept up a veneer of toughness that scared most of her classmates away. Only Tracey and Emily hadn't been put off by her attitude. They got to know the real Jenna, and they accepted her.

So Jenna really hoped she hadn't hurt Emily's feelings, and just to find out, she searched Emily's thoughts. It was never easy reading Emily's mind—with all those premonitions and visions, it was kind of cluttered. It was easier to figure out what Emily was *feeling*—Jenna could almost always get a sense of that.

Actually, Jenna sometimes found it difficult reading the minds of everyone in this class, especially Madame. Probably because none of them was completely normal.

But she got enough from Emily to reassure herself that Emily wasn't brooding on Jenna's teasing. Emily—like Jenna—was wondering where all the missing students were.

So was Madame, apparently. The teacher looked seriously disturbed as she surveyed the room.

"I'm going to the principal's office," she announced. "I want you all to spend the time writing down your own personal goals for your gifts."

This wasn't an unusual assignment. Madame frequently ordered them to ponder their gifts and note their thoughts. But this time, she looked like her own thoughts were elsewhere.

She left the room, and Jenna turned to Ken sitting next to her. The dark-haired, broad-shouldered former athlete seemed lost in his own thoughts, which wasn't unusual either. He was a friendly guy, but he always looked like something was bothering him.

"What's going on?" she asked him. "Where do you think they are?"

Ken gave his head a little shake, as if he was trying to lose whatever was occupying his mind. Or maybe he was just responding to her question.

"Not a clue," he replied. "Can you read their minds?"

Jenna didn't think so. Every now and then, if someone was trying to be heard, she could read minds from a distance. But usually she had to be in close proximity to the person.

"I'll try," she said. She closed her eyes and envisioned Carter, Tracey, and Martin. Nothing came to her.

"They're not trying to contact me," she told Ken.

"Me neither," Ken said.

Jenna was relieved to hear this, since only dead people talked to Ken. She looked around at the others in the room. Emily was still staring into space, probably trying to drum up visions, which was a good thing, Jenna suspected. She didn't want to disturb her.

Off to the side of the room in his wheelchair, Charles seemed to be trying to amuse himself. Two pencils, engaged in what looked like a sword fight and unguided by any hands, floated in the air in front of him. Clearly Charles was moving them with his mind. *He* didn't appear to be concerned about the missing students. That made sense, since Charles rarely thought about anyone but himself—which was probably why he didn't have a friend in the world.

Sarah was doing what she was supposed to be doing. She had her class notebook open on her desk and was writing studiously. Jenna didn't bother to read her mind. Sarah seemed to avoid thinking anything interesting in case she felt tempted to use her gift.

Amanda was fidgeting. She rapped her fingernails on her desk, opened and closed her notebook, and tapped a foot. Finally, she got up and went over to Ken, the one person in the class she felt was on her social level and therefore worth communicating with.

"This is creepy," she declared.

"No kidding," Jenna remarked.

Amanda shot her a quick withering look as if to say "I wasn't talking to you." Jenna didn't care. Having hung out with Amanda when Amanda was occupying Tracey's body, she knew that she was a mass of contradictions—inside, she was actually sort of decent. But her mean-girl act wasn't just on the surface. It went pretty deep, and sometimes Amanda could be sincerely nasty.

Never to Ken though. Even if he wasn't involved in sports anymore, he'd been a total jock before his accident, and that obviously counted for a lot in Amanda's book. Jenna often suspected Amanda had a crush on him.

"What do *you* think, Ken?" Amanda asked.

"Something's going on," Ken said. "If they were sick, they'd be on the absentee list. Their parents must be worried."

"Carter doesn't have any parents," Amanda pointed out. "And Tracey's parents probably think she's vanished on purpose. But if Martin's parents don't know where he is, they have to be going crazy. He used to live across the street from me, and I remember his mother always calling for him to come in if he was out playing."

Jenna couldn't resist. "So you and Martin played together as children?" she asked mischievously. "Were you like best friends?"

Amanda didn't even dignify that with a reply. "Ken, what do you think we should do?"

"I don't know," Ken said simply.

Jenna had a suggestion. "We could ask Emily who's going to vanish next." She turned to Ken. "Emily predicted that Carter and Tracey and Martin would disappear."

Ken's eyebrows went up. "Yeah? Hey, Emily." He raised his voice. "Emily!"

Slowly, Emily turned to them. "Yes?"

"Come here," Amanda said imperiously.

Don't take orders from her, Emily, Jenna thought furiously. But Emily wasn't a mind reader, and she still looked so dazed, she'd probably take orders from a squirrel.

She made her way over to Jenna, Ken, and Amanda.

"What's going on?" Amanda demanded to know.

Emily was taken aback. "How would I know?"

Ken spoke much more kindly. "Did you have a premonition that those three would disappear?"

Emily nodded. "Yes. But that's all I saw. Just them not being here."

Amanda sniffed. "That's *all*? Oh, great. You see people missing—big deal. What good is your gift, Emily, if you don't know why they're gone or where they are or anything?"

Jenna was glad to see that Emily was now getting annoyed with Miss I'm-All-That. "Sorry if my gift doesn't meet your high standards of—of *giftedness*, Amanda."

Jenna clapped her hands in glee and Ken grinned.

But Amanda was not pleased. Her voice rose. "You know what I think, Emily? You're just showing off. You didn't even have any premonitions."

"Oh yes she did," Jenna interjected.

Amanda ignored that. "You're a great big fake, Emily."

Emily drew herself up. "I am *not*."

Now Amanda's voice became shrill. "Oh yeah? Then tell us who's going to disappear next!"

Now Jenna understood. Amanda was getting nervous.

Emily looked directly into Amanda's eyes. "You are."

It was all Jenna could do to keep herself from patting Emily on the back to congratulate her. This was exactly what Amanda needed to hear— something that would make her freak out. She deserved to be frightened.

And she was scared—anyone could see that. She went completely pale, and given the amount of makeup she used, that was pretty dramatic. And her thoughts were so clear to Jenna that she was surprised everyone couldn't hear them.

Ohmigod ohmigod ohmigod what am I going to do, help me, somebody, help me . . .

And then Amanda ran out of the room, looking as if she was about to throw up.

"That wasn't very nice, Emily," Ken said.

"I couldn't help it," Emily said simply. She turned and went back to her seat.

"It served Amanda right," Jenna said to Ken. "She can be pretty nasty."

Ken shrugged. He'd been distracted by a new game Charles was playing on the other side of the room. Charles was sending things into the wastebasket next to Madame's desk. First, he threw a crumpled piece of paper. It sailed through the air and landed in the basket. Then he crumpled another piece of paper and did the same thing.

"It's amazing, what that guy can do with his mind," Ken said. But Jenna thought it was a waste of a gift to use it on stupid activities like that.

When he got bored, Charles looked around for something more interesting to toss.

"Charles, stop it!" Sarah cried out as her bag

suddenly left her side and went sailing through the air in the direction of the wastebasket.

Why didn't Sarah just *make* him stop? Jenna wondered. She knew why, of course. Because Sarah refused to use her power. What Jenna really wondered was *why* she wouldn't use it. As with Ken, there was something secretive about Sarah.

Now Sarah's bag hung in midair, upside down, and all the contents poured out into the wastebasket.

"Charles!" Sarah wailed.

"Cut it out, Charles," Ken said, but Charles ignored him. Jenna glared at him in disgust.

"You're such a jerk, Charles. No wonder you don't have any friends."

"Who says I don't have any friends?"

"It's pretty obvious," Jenna retorted. "You're always alone. I think that speaks for itself."

Luckily for Sarah, Madame returned to the room then. She saw Sarah's bag fall into the wastebasket, and no one had to tell her what was going on.

"*Charles*," she said.

For a second, Charles faked a look of innocence. Then, with a shrug, he looked in the direction of the wastebasket. Sarah's bag rose out of it and returned to Sarah's desk.

Madame didn't say anything else to Charles. She didn't even threaten him with demerits, as she normally would have done. Jenna didn't try to read her mind—she knew from experience that it was impossible to know what Madame was thinking.

The bell rang, and Madame didn't even mention the assignment she'd given them. "Have a nice day," she said automatically as they all got up and headed for the door. But as Jenna passed Madame's desk, she thought she heard an additional remark from the teacher.

It sounded like, "Be careful."

CHAPTER FOUR

THE NEXT DAY AT school, Emily found it even harder than usual to concentrate in her classes. She was feeling just a little bit ashamed of herself. Maybe more than a little. What she'd said to Amanda—telling her she would be the next one to vanish—wasn't very nice. She knew Jenna was proud of her for having the guts to talk to Amanda like that, but it wasn't really an Emily thing to do. She wasn't the type to fight mean with mean.

Amanda had been really scared, Emily knew. She'd probably worried about it all night long. She might not even be at school today, she was so nervous. But if she wasn't there, it wouldn't be because of Emily's prediction. Because it hadn't been Amanda who was missing in Emily's most recent vision of the gifted class.

She'd had the vision before Amanda even called

her over in class the previous day. It came just after Madame left the classroom to make phone calls; it came without any effort on her part. She hadn't even forced her eyes to glaze over—it happened automatically.

The vision had been the clearest one yet. There was the gifted class, on the next day—today. She was positive about the date, because she could actually make out the calendar that hung by the door. *That* was peculiar—her visions didn't usually include details like that. She could easily see that Carter still wasn't there, and neither were Tracey and Martin. And there was another person missing.

Sarah.

She confessed this to Jenna at lunch. "I don't know why I didn't warn Sarah. Maybe I just wasn't sure it was a real prediction. Or maybe I guess I just didn't want to scare her."

Jenna grinned. "Yeah, scaring Amanda is much more fun."

"*Jenna.*"

"Oh, c'mon, Em—lighten up. It was good for

Amanda. She's got a little too much self-esteem. She needs to be taken down a notch."

Emily looked over at another table in the cafeteria. "She doesn't look upset today."

Amanda was with her usual snotty friends at their usual table. Nina was crying, she noticed. She must have just found out she didn't make the cheerleading squad. The other girls looked like they were comforting her. Not Amanda though. She was busy filing her fingernails. She couldn't even show a little sympathy for her own friend! Maybe Jenna was right. Amanda deserved a scare, even if it didn't last very long.

Jenna was eating. "You know, these school lunches aren't half bad. The way you and Tracey are always complaining, I thought they'd be a lot worse."

"Speaking of Tracey," Emily said, "aren't you just a little worried about her?"

"Not really. Because I still think Tracey disappeared on purpose. You know how she's been trying for ages to stay invisible for longer periods."

"What about Carter and Martin?"

"Well, Carter's a mystery, right? He appeared out

of nowhere, and now he's disappeared. I just can't get too spooked by him. And Martin, he's always whining about his home and how his mother nags him. He probably ran away. Any day now, they'll find him sleeping in a bus station."

"So you still don't believe in my predictions."

Jenna just shrugged. "You said it yourself—they're pretty screwed up."

Emily didn't get it. "But you supported me yesterday in front of Ken and Amanda."

"I'm your friend," Jenna said matter-of-factly. "I'm always loyal to my friends." She went back to her mashed potatoes. "Could you pass the salt?"

Emily couldn't believe Jenna could be so blithe about everything. She wished she could read her friend's mind. She had a pretty good feeling this was all an act Jenna was putting on, to show how tough she was.

"What about Sarah?"

Jenna did her who-cares shrug. "Let's wait and see if she shows up in class."

She didn't. The second Emily entered room 209, her heart sank when she saw the empty seat. Sarah was always there early. Madame, at her desk, was staring at Sarah's seat, too.

Ken arrived, then Amanda, then Charles. Jenna sauntered in as the bell rang. When she saw Sarah's empty seat, she turned to Emily.

"Okay, I take it back. You've got a gift."

Madame spoke sharply. "What do you mean by that, Jenna?"

Madame was one of the only people who could intimidate Jenna, and Jenna practically stammered. "Well, I, uh, meant that, you know, how Emily makes predictions of the future, and, you know . . ."

Madame broke in. "Emily! Did you know that Sarah would disappear?"

Emily shifted uneasily in her seat. "I—I sort of had a vision. But I didn't know if it was real."

Madame stared at her. "And the others? Carter, Tracey, Martin—did you have visions about them?"

Suddenly Emily felt terrible. She nodded.

"Why didn't you say anything?"

"Because—because I didn't trust them. The visions, I mean. My predictions are always so mixed-up. They're like bits and pieces, like a puzzle, and

I can't put them together to make a real picture! Like, I'll see an earthquake, but I don't know when or where it's going to happen. Or I'll see someone have an accident in gymnastics, but I don't know if it's going to be at the next competition or the one after that."

It dawned on her that she'd probably never said so much at one time in class.

Madame looked sad. "I know your premonitions are confusing, Emily. But you have a gift. You should have told me about these visions."

Not for the first time, Emily wished she could give her gift back to whomever gave it to her. The disappointment in Madame's face . . . Emily couldn't bear to look at her teacher. She felt like she'd let her down. Not to mention Carter and the other missing students.

Madame's voice became softer. "There's always an element of truth in your visions, Emily. You might not understand them, but they have meaning. You have to learn how to interpret them, to look for clues that can help you put them in context. You have to figure out what's important and weed out what's irrelevant."

Emily's head was hurting, and her eyes were stinging.

"Can you see them, Emily?" Madame asked. "The missing students . . . Can you see where they are? Is anything coming to you?"

Emily shook her head. "I see the future, not the present," she whispered.

"Concentrate on the future of one of them," Madame urged. "Carter. Do you see him in the future?"

She tried very, very hard, so hard her head wasn't just hurting, it was throbbing. Something started happening. A blurry image began to form . . .

In pain, she managed to say, "I see him, I see him."

"Where is he?" Madame asked.

"Here. He's here, in class, in his seat."

"And the others?" Madame persisted. "Where are they?"

Her head was about to explode. Emily burst into tears. "I don't know, I don't know."

She was dimly aware of Jenna on one side of her,

Madame on the other. As they led her out of the room, Madame spoke softly.

"I'm sorry, Emily, I shouldn't have pushed you like that. I'm going to send you to the infirmary and have your mother called. Jenna, could you go with her?"

A short time later, Emily was lying on the infirmary cot, and the school nurse was calling her mother. And it wasn't long until her mother appeared at the door.

"The school called me. Honey, are you all right?" She came to the cot and put a hand on Emily's forehead. Emily gently pushed it away.

"I don't have a fever, Mom."

"She just got upset in class," Jenna declared. "Madame thought she should go home."

Her mother's lips tightened. "Which class? The crazy class?"

"Mom!" Emily shot Jenna an apologetic look.

"It's okay," Jenna murmured. "I'd better get back."

Emily's mother didn't even bother to thank her for helping Emily. She was more than upset.

"I'm taking you out of that class," she declared in

the car on the way home. "It's not doing you any good at all—it's making things worse. Now, you just close your eyes and relax. I'll give you some aspirin when we get home."

Emily was grateful to be left alone. She had a lot to think about.

She'd tried to tell Madame about her visions, and she should have tried again. But Madame just kept telling her she needed to interpret them, to study them, and never told Emily *how*. Was she stupid? Or lazy? Now she was starting to feel like she'd been given a gift she didn't deserve. Carter, Tracey, Martin, and Sarah . . . With her gift, she might have been able to stop them from disappearing. If only she'd worked harder, if only she'd understood what her visions meant . . . Now her head was hurting again, but she was glad. She deserved the pain. She'd never felt so guilty in her life.

At home, she swallowed the pills her mother brought her, even though she knew they wouldn't do any good. But they did help her to relax a little, and maybe that was why the vision appeared.

She saw herself, in the dark of night, on a street

corner. She could read the names on the signpost—Maple Street and Stewart Avenue. She wore jeans, a green T-shirt, and a brown sweater. She was alone.

A car pulled up. With no street lights, she couldn't see what color it was, but she could tell it was an ordinary car, nothing fancy or unusual. There was a woman in the driver's seat and a man sitting next to her. The woman's hair was blond—it must have been a very light blond for Emily to be able to notice it in the darkness.

One of them said something. She couldn't hear the words, but the Emily in her vision got into the car. And then the vision faded.

Emily sat up. *How bizarre*, she thought. She knew Stewart Avenue—it was on the other side of town, in a business district that was busy by day, empty at night. What possible reason would she have to go there? And why would she get into a car with strangers? For as long as she could remember, her mother had warned her never to talk to strangers, let alone get into a car with them. It was the wrong thing to do. Didn't all parents warn their children about this? Anyone with half a brain knew how dangerous talking to strangers could be. It was totally out of character for her to even daydream of doing something stupid like that.

She took the book she'd been reading from her nightstand and opened it. It was a good book, a mystery, and she looked forward to reading a few pages every night before going to bed. But she couldn't concentrate on it. She got up and went out to the living room.

Her mother was watching TV. She was pleased to see Emily. "Are you feeling better, honey? Do you want something to eat?"

Emily shook her head. "I'm not hungry, Mom. But I'm not sick," she added hastily.

"How about if I heat up the leftover macaroni and cheese?" her mother asked hopefully.

She knew that if she could show some enthusiasm for macaroni and cheese, her mother would feel a lot better.

"Okay, that would be great."

Soon she and her mother were curled up on the sofa with bowls of macaroni and cheese. They found a marathon of a fashion makeover reality show on TV and settled down for the evening.

Emily liked this kind of show. She enjoyed watching ugly ducklings turn into swans with the right clothes and makeup. But no matter how entertaining the episodes were, her mind kept going back to that last strange vision. Maple and Stewart. When would she find herself on the corner of Maple and Stewart? And why?

By ten thirty, both she and her mother were yawning and the marathon was finished. Her mother did something she hadn't done in years—she followed Emily into her bedroom to tuck her in.

"I know you're going to feel better in the morning," she said, kissing Emily on the forehead. "And I'm going to call your principal. You won't have to go to that gifted class anymore."

Emily was in no mood to argue. "'Night, Mom."

Once her mother left, she realized she really wasn't sleepy at all. She just lay there and thought about the events of the past week. But there, in the corner of her mind, she kept going back to that earlier vision. Maple and Stewart, Maple and Stewart . . .

She gave up on trying to sleep, got out of bed, and went to her desk. Madame was always telling her she had to interpret the visions, search for details and look for clues. So once her computer had warmed up, she typed "Maple and Stewart" into the search box on her Internet browser and hit enter.

There was an old movie starring actors named Alicia Maple and Del Stewart, and a store called Maple and Stewart that sold plumbing supplies. There was a law firm called Maple, Stewart and Jones, and a mapping service that offered to give her directions to the corner of Maple and Stewart. She clicked on that one, but it didn't tell her anything she didn't already know.

There were no clues here.

Maple and Stewart . . . She realized the street intersection wasn't far from where Jenna lived in that housing project. Maybe Jenna would know something unusual about that corner. She looked at the clock. It was after eleven, too late to call. But there was a chance Jenna might be up late surfing on her computer. Emily could send an instant message. She went into her e-mail file, where Jenna was listed as an IM friend, but she wasn't online.

She noticed something else though—a notification that she had a new e-mail. She clicked on it.

Hi Emily, it's me, Tracey. I'm so sorry—they made me send this. They said they'd hurt us if I didn't. Can you go to the corner of Maple and Stewart tonight at midnight and wait there? Someone will pick you up.

Tracey

And then someone had added, a couple of lines down:

If you want to find your classmates, you will be there.

And find herself in the same danger her classmates were probably in. But it was her fault if her classmates were in danger. She knew what she had to do.

In the dim light, she dressed in the same clothes she'd been wearing in her vision: jeans and a green T-shirt. The brown sweater hung on the back of her chair. She threw a few things in her backpack— her contact lens case, a change of underwear, her toothbrush. And she put her watch back on.

She scribbled a note and placed it on her bed. Then she left the room, glancing anxiously at the half closed door to her mother's bedroom. She noted with relief that there was no light on—her mother wasn't up reading. Even so, she moved very quietly. Her mother was a light sleeper.

Once outside, she debated taking her bike, which was in the building's parking garage. But she had plenty of time to get there by midnight, so she went on foot. It took her forty-five minutes to reach the corner of Maple and Stewart.

There were no lights, no sounds—the area was deserted, just like in her vision. It was a little chilly—maybe she should have worn a jacket. But she hadn't been wearing a jacket in the vision.

She waited. Funnily enough, she didn't feel very nervous. In fact, she was unusually calm. She looked at her watch. It was midnight.

She heard something and looked down the street. In the distance, she could see a car coming. It wasn't going very fast.

She couldn't make out the color of the car, but it looked fairly ordinary. It slowed down as it approached her corner and then stopped. There was a blond haired woman in the driver's seat and a man next to her. Shadows obscured their faces, but the woman's platinum blond hair was too bright to ignore.

The woman spoke, calmly but firmly. "Get in, Emily."

She did. Because she knew that in this particular situation, it was the right thing to do.

CHAPTER FIVE

J ENNA WAS ANXIOUS TO talk to Ken, and when she spotted him on the steps leading to the school entrance, she hurried toward him. But when she reached the bottom of the steps, she paused. She could see who he was with, and there was no way she could talk to Ken now. He was with a couple of jocks, and not just ordinary athletes. They were stars—even Jenna, who was not into sports, recognized them as the cocaptains of Meadowbrook's basketball team. She'd been forced to go to assemblies where these guys had been introduced and cheered, along with the football, soccer, and baseball captains.

Jenna had very firm opinions about jocks—as far as she was concerned, they were all stupid and boring. Emily and Tracey always told her this was a stereotype and couldn't possibly be true of every athlete in the world, but Jenna held firmly to her beliefs. There was no way she wanted those guys to hear the news she had for Ken.

She couldn't understand why Ken hung around guys like that, even though Ken himself had been a major jock once, before she came to Meadowbrook. Emily had told her he was captain of the soccer team, and he'd been injured in a bad accident. In fact, according to Emily, it was just after the accident that he developed his gift. And Ken was okay—not boring and definitely not stupid. So maybe her attitude toward athletes really was a stereotype.

Still, her news was private and personal and only for Ken's ears. But it was getting close to the time when they'd all have to enter the building. Ken would be off to his first class, and she'd lose this opportunity to talk to him. So she slowly mounted the steps and edged toward the boys. Somehow she had to get Ken away from his buddies.

She was close enough to hear Ken now. It sounded like he was congratulating the other two.

"That was an amazing game last night."

"Incredible," one of the boys said. He cocked his head toward the taller boy. "When Mike made that first basket, I was totally blown away. It looked like a wild throw to me."

"It was a wild throw," Mike admitted. "I was as shocked as everyone else when it cleared the net."

"You were lucky," Ken remarked.

"Yeah," Mike agreed. "And I stayed lucky all night. I didn't miss a throw."

"It couldn't be just luck," the other boy said. "You were terrific at Monday's game, too."

"I know," Mike said, but his forehead puckered. "I don't know what happened. I haven't been that good all season."

"No kidding," the other boy said. "You've been a disaster. I don't think you scored half a dozen points before Monday." He turned to Ken. "You should have heard the way Coach has been bawling him out."

"So that's what got you going," Ken commented.

"I guess," Mike said, but he didn't sound very sure of himself. "Hey, Ken . . . you know that kid in the wheelchair?"

"Charles Temple? Yeah, what about him?"

"He was at the game last night."

"So what?" the other boy asked.

"He was at Monday's game, too. I noticed because of the wheelchair—he couldn't go up into the stands. He was on the floor, just at the edge of the court."

Ken echoed the other boy. "So what?"

Mike looked distinctly uncomfortable. "I don't know. I never saw him at a game before. And he kept giving me weird looks. There's something spooky about him."

Now Ken looked uncomfortable. "Spooky?"

"Yeah . . . You know anything about him?"

"No." Ken noticed Jenna on the lower step. "Uh, I gotta go talk to that girl. See you guys."

He hurried down the stairs and joined Jenna. "Did you hear those guys? Geez, I hate when people ask me about the gifted group."

Jenna had more important things on her mind. "Listen, something's happened. Emily's gone."

He looked at her blankly. "Gone where?" Then his eyes widened. "You mean, she's disappeared like the others?"

"Not exactly. She left a note for her mother, so she didn't just disappear—she knew she was going away. Her mother called me this morning. She was completely hysterical."

"Did the note say where she went?"

Jenna shook her head. "Only something about how she had to find her friends and not to worry about her."

"But how would she know where to look for them?"

"I don't know. Maybe she had a vision. We should find Madame and tell her."

That turned out to be unnecessary. Once inside the building, they were witness to a commotion going on just outside the principal's office. Madame's calm, measured tone could be heard, but Emily's mother's angry voice was louder.

"How can you let this happen?" she cried. "Young people start disappearing from one particular class and parents aren't notified?"

Madame replied, "The parents of the missing students were notified immediately, Mrs. Sanders."

Emily's mother wasn't satisfied with that. "And what about the parents of the other students? If I'd known what was happening in that so-called gifted class, I could have prevented my daughter's disappearance!"

Other kids had been attracted by the noise and were gathering around. The principal, Mr. Jackson, looked nervous. He ushered the two women into his office and closed the door.

By the time the bell rang for homeroom, word of all the missing students had spread through the school. Homeroom classmates who knew that Jenna was in the gifted class gave her uneasy looks, like they half-expected her to vanish before their very eyes. Jenna didn't care about that—with her goth makeup, black clothes, and tough-girl attitude, she was used to being stared at. But she cared about her friends, Tracey and Emily, and she was even worried about the classmates she wasn't so friendly with. She looked forward to class and the opportunity to talk with Madame and the remaining students about what they could do.

She didn't have to wait for the class. Before homeroom was over, the teacher received a note and beckoned to Jenna.

"You're to go to room 209 immediately," the teacher told her.

When Jenna arrived, Amanda was the only other of her gifted classmates in the room.

"Do you know why we're meeting now?" Jenna asked her.

Amanda shrugged.

"Is it about Emily?"

Amanda just shrugged again. Jenna gazed at her curiously.

"Have you even heard about Emily?"

"No."

"She's missing. I think she ran away to look for the other students."

"What other students?"

"The ones who disappeared from our class!"

Amanda nodded. "Okay," she said. She rose from her chair and started toward the door. Jenna blocked her. She hadn't expected Amanda to show any deep concern about this, but not getting any reaction at all surprised her.

"Amanda! C'mon, we have to talk about this, we have to do something."

Amanda looked at her blankly. "Why?"

Now Jenna was shocked. None of Amanda's friends could hear them, so there was no reason for her to put on an act. And she knew Amanda had some decent qualities, some real feelings. This total lack of interest was very, very strange.

Unless . . . unless . . . "You're the other Amanda," Jenna declared, her heart sinking.

The real Amanda would have snapped at Jenna and called her crazy. This Amanda simply stared at her blankly.

Jenna sighed. "Sit down, Amanda."

The Other-Amanda obeyed.

There was no point in trying to talk to this whatever-it-was, this thing that looked like Amanda, talked like Amanda, moved like Amanda—but wasn't Amanda, just a robotic shell of the real girl. Oh, what a crummy time for Amanda to suddenly do a body snatch! She might not have the world's best personality, but at least she was smart.

Which was probably why she'd done a body snatch. She must have really believed Emily's prediction. Which clearly didn't come true, since the body of Amanda was still here. But where was the real Amanda?

So there was only herself, Ken, and Charles left to work with Madame on this situation. Ken was the next to arrive.

"I just saw Madame," he said. "She's going to be a little late. The police are here, and she has to talk to them."

Jenna shook her head. "I don't think the police are going to be much help. You know these aren't regular kidnappings. There won't be ransom demands or anything like that."

"You're right." Ken turned to Amanda. "Hi, Amanda. You got any theories about this?"

"About what?"

"The missing students! Jenna and I were just saying we don't think these are ordinary kidnappings."

Other-Amanda opened her handbag and brought out a cosmetic case. She set up a little mirror on her desk and began applying mascara to her eyelashes.

"Amanda!" Ken said again. "Do you have any ideas?"

"No," she replied and continued putting on her makeup.

"Don't bother with her," Jenna informed him. "She's not Amanda."

Ken understood what she meant and groaned. "Oh, no."

Madame arrived. Despite the events of the morning, she seemed calm, though Jenna thought she detected a dark glint in the teacher's eyes. She didn't waste any time on opening remarks.

"We have a situation," she said abruptly. "And we've all got to work together." She stopped. "Where's Charles?"

As if on cue, the door opened and Charles wheeled himself in. "Sorry I'm late," he said casually. "I was hanging with my friends."

"What friends?" Ken murmured.

"Could I have *everyone's* attention?" Madame demanded. "Amanda?"

"She's not Amanda, Madame," Jenna told her.

The teacher sighed and closed her eyes for a moment as if trying to absorb this new bad news.

"All right, thank you, Jenna. Charles, would you please stop that immediately!"

Jenna realized that paper clips were jumping out of the tray on Madame's desk and going into the cup that held pencils and pens. But Madame had spoken more sharply than usual, and Charles stopped.

Madame continued in the same tone. "We can't afford not to take this seriously, people! I do not believe that Tracey is invisible or that Martin has run away from home. Someone—some organization—is causing members of our class to disappear, and these disappearances have something to do with who you are. We have to figure out who is behind this and why."

"Do you think they're in danger?" Ken asked the teacher.

"It's quite possible, though not in the way you think. I don't think they will be physically injured. But I do think they will be used."

Jenna knew what she meant. It was Madame's greatest fear for them—that their gifts could be utilized by people with bad intentions. Trust no one—that was her mantra. But Madame's next comment surprised her.

"I must say, though, I feel a little better knowing that Emily has gone in search of them."

Jenna's mouth fell open. "Why?"

"Because in a situation like this, I think she's our best hope," Madame said simply.

Jenna couldn't believe what she was hearing. Emily, their best hope? Emily, with her inaccurate predictions? Emily, whose gift was the weakest of them all?

If Emily was their best hope, Jenna thought, then they were in more trouble than she'd ever imagined.

Chapter Six

WHEN SHE WOKE UP, Emily had no idea where she was—geographically speaking. She could tell that she was in a bed, but that was about it.

Immediately after she'd entered the back seat of the car, the man in the passenger's seat turned around, leaned toward her, and put a blindfold over her eyes. He'd done this gently, almost apologetically, but even so it had been a frightening moment, and Emily had started to panic. This wasn't alleviated by the woman's sharp voice.

"Don't struggle, Emily. There's nothing you can do."

"What's going on?" Emily asked, without much hope of getting an answer.

"You'll find out when the time is right," the woman said.

The man spoke in a kinder tone. "Here's something to drink."

She felt a bottle being placed in her hand. Then she heard a soft whirring sound. Reaching out, she felt a glass panel that now separated her from the people in the front seat, like in a limousine. She wouldn't be able to hear anything they said to each other.

There was one benefit to the silence and darkness. It might be easier to concentrate and envision her future. She took a sip from the bottle and almost immediately wanted to kick herself. *How stupid can I be?* she wondered as drowsiness swept over her.

Now, awake, she sat up in the bed. There was nothing covering her eyes, but the room was pitch-dark. She could feel a table next to her bed and something that could be a lamp on it. By touch, she located a button and pushed it in.

Light flooded the room. There wasn't much to see though. It was a plain room, with light blue walls. There was something on one wall in the shape of a window, but it was completely covered by a metal shutter. A white chest of drawers stood against the far wall.

There were two other beds in the room, but both were empty. They were unmade and looked as if they'd been slept in recently. The door started to open, and Emily stiffened.

"Good morning."

Emily let out the breath she'd been holding. "Tracey."

Tracey came over and sat on the edge of Emily's bed. "How are you feeling?"

"A little groggy," Emily admitted.

Tracey nodded. "They gave you something to make you out of it."

"Where are we?"

"I don't know," Tracey replied. "In some kind of house, but I don't know the address. And all the windows are blocked."

"How did they get you here?"

"They grabbed me inside the girls' bathroom at school and put a wet towel on my face. There must have been something in it that knocked me out.

They must have put me in a car and taken me here. I woke up in this room."

"A man and a woman with blond hair?"

Tracey shook her head. "There were two men, and the woman was a redhead."

So there were at least four of them, Emily thought. "Who are they?"

"I don't know."

"What do they want us for?"

"I don't know that either."

"Tracey!" Emily exclaimed in frustration. "You've been here three days. Haven't you learned anything?"

She shook her head. "Nothing. I managed to go invisible on the first night and looked around the place, but I couldn't find any clues. There's a floor above us, but the door at the top of the stairway is locked. I guess that's where they stay."

A creak above them confirmed this. Someone was up there.

"I think they know about my gift," Tracey continued. "Even when I'm invisible, they whisper to each other and I can't hear a word they're saying."

"Did you try just asking them what they want?"

"Of course I asked them," Tracey said. "They just keep saying I have to be patient. Maybe they're waiting till they have us all here before they explain what they want." She offered a half-hearted smile. "No offense, but I was hoping the next captive would be Jenna. At least she might be able to read their minds and figure out what's going on."

"I can't believe you're being so calm about this," Emily marveled.

Tracey shrugged. "Someone has to be calm. Carter's worthless, of course. He's just like he is back at school. He does what he's told, and the rest of the time he stares into space. Martin whimpers and whines. Sarah looks totally freaked and barely speaks. I think maybe she's in shock."

"I can relate to that," Emily said with feeling. "Do they know about all our gifts?"

"I don't know!" Tracey replied for the umpteenth time. Then she looked sadly at Emily. "I'm sorry I dragged you into this. They made me write that message to you."

"I didn't care. I wanted to help all of you. I felt

bad that I didn't see what was going to happen in time. I could have warned you."

"Don't be such a goof. You couldn't have stopped them."

Emily's stomach rumbled loudly.

"You're hungry," Tracey declared. "Get dressed and we'll have some breakfast. I have to say, they're taking pretty good care of us here. The food's okay, and there's lots of entertainment."

"It's still a prison," Emily reminded her as she got into the sweatpants and shirt that were laid out on the bed.

"Well, at least it's an upscale one," Tracey said. "There are DVDs, an Xbox, games . . ." She was still extolling the virtues of their jail as Emily followed her out of the bedroom.

Emily wasn't fooled by Tracey's cheery tone. This was a Tracey thing to do—take charge and try to keep their spirits up. Clearly this wasn't working for Martin. Entering what appeared to be a dining room, they found him slumped in his seat, eyeing his plate of food mournfully.

"I like my eggs sunny-side up," he whined.

"Shut up and eat," Tracey ordered him. "Scrambled eggs are just as good. And look at that nice crispy bacon."

Carter ate steadily, but the expression on his face—or lack of expression—gave no indication of whether or not he was enjoying the food. Sarah looked exactly like Tracey had described her—just plain scared.

Remembering the drink in the car, Emily eyed the food warily. But Tracey had said it was okay, and there was Carter, not showing any side effects from eating it. Along with the eggs and bacon, there was toast and orange juice that looked freshly squeezed. Emily didn't think she'd be able to eat, but she surprised herself.

Maybe it was because the place just didn't seem scary at all. Except for the lack of windows, they could have been in any normal, ordinary house. They sat around a big table on comfortable, matching chairs. The plates were decorated with a floral pattern, similar to the dinnerware Emily knew at home. There were real forks, knives, and spoons, not plastic ones.

Surreptitiously Emily touched the edge of the knife lightly. No, it wasn't sharp enough to cut anything tougher than eggs. Not that she'd ever have the guts to stab a human being . . .

From what Emily remembered from the night before, they hadn't behaved like serious bad guys. The woman wasn't friendly, but she hadn't been nasty, and the man was almost nice.

She was pretty sure it was the same man who entered the dining room at that moment. He was thin, slightly balding, with a neatly trimmed short beard and wire-rimmed glasses perched on his nose. As he approached the table, everyone froze and looked at him.

He placed a stack of napkins on the table. "Do you need anything?" he asked the group in general. "I suppose you're too young for coffee."

He wasn't frightening at all. In fact, as he gazed around the table, he looked a little uncomfortable, almost nervous.

No one said anything. "I can make more toast if you want it," he offered. When none of them asked for any, he left the room looking relieved.

As she continued eating, Emily noticed a tear trickling down Sarah's face. Tracey must have noticed it, too. Sitting next to Sarah, she leaned over and put an arm around her shoulders.

"It's going to be okay," she said soothingly.

Sarah flinched and shrugged off Tracey's arm. "Get off."

Emily eyed her curiously. She didn't know Sarah well at all, but she was always nice in class, never rude. Clearly the situation was affecting her. She just hoped that meant Sarah would use her gift if it became absolutely necessary.

They were all finishing their breakfast now. Again Tracey took charge.

"Who wants to go into the living room and play *Grand Theft Auto?*" she asked brightly.

No one jumped at the opportunity, and it didn't matter anyway, because at that moment the hostage-takers or kidnappers or whatever they were all entered the dining room. There was the balding guy and another guy with a lot of curly brown hair who was shorter and fat. While the skinny guy still looked nervous, the shorter one was grinning. They weren't young but they weren't old. Emily guessed they were around her mother's age.

It was the woman who really grabbed her attention. For one thing, she was very pretty, sort of glamorous looking. Emily estimated her age at around thirty, but she wore a lot of makeup so it was hard to tell. She wore fashionable tight jeans with boots and a polka-dot shirt. Her long black hair gleamed with midnight-blue highlights, and she wore hoop earrings that looked like real gold.

Her eyes were blue, but a very different shade of blue than the streaks in her hair. They were so pale they were practically transparent.

What was really amazing was her expression—or, more accurately, her lack of expression. Her perfectly sculpted features were completely blank. For a second, her lips stretched and turned up slightly at the ends, but never in a million years would Emily have called that a smile. If anything, it made her shiver.

"Welcome," she said, although there was nothing welcoming about her flat voice. "I hope you're all comfortable. My name is Clare." She indicated the chubby guy. "This is Howard, and the man on my other side is George."

George looked at the ground and murmured, "Hello." Howard beamed at them. "Hi, guys!"

Now she was positive George was the man who'd been in the back seat with her. But she wasn't sure about the woman. The voice sounded familiar, and she could be wearing a wig. Or last night's blond hair was a wig. Or the red hair Tracey had seen . . . Oh, why was she thinking about hair at a time like this?

Clare continued. "I know this must be strange to you, and you have to be wondering what's going on. Well, now that you're all here, we can explain."

Emily looked at Tracey and knew she had to be thinking the same thing. If the point had been to kidnap all the gifted students, then they weren't all here.

The woman might have been a mind reader. "We're not bringing in all your classmates, by the way. You're the ones we need now."

Tracey spoke up. "Why?"

"For your gifts, of course." The odd lip twitch

which must have been her version of a smile appeared briefly again. "You're all exceptional young people with very special talents. Tracey, you can become invisible. Martin, you're capable of great strength. Emily, you have the ability to see the future, and Sarah . . . Sarah, you have the greatest gift of all. You can control people."

Emily shuddered. She sounded so matter-of-fact, she could have been talking about who excelled at math and who could play the piano. Maybe this was why she seemed scarier than the men. There was something unreal about her.

As scared as she was, Emily had to say something, and she said the first thing that came to mind.

"What about Carter? He doesn't have a gift."

Clare didn't seem surprised, and she only glanced at Carter, almost as if he was insignificant. "That doesn't matter. We've got the people we need."

Again, Emily was amazed at her own daring. "The people you need for what?"

The pale blue eyes rested on her. "You're going to help us rob a bank."

Chapter Seven

This turned out to be all the information they were going to get for the moment. The group was dismissed, with Clare's promise that they'd learn more at lunchtime. Emily followed the others into what they called the living room.

Tracey hadn't been exaggerating when she described the amusements available in their prison. The room was like a massive media center, with a large flat-screen TV, video game equipment, computers, and iPods with headsets for anyone who wanted to listen to music. A bookcase held books (all the latest teen series), DVDs, video games, board games . . . everything and anything remotely entertaining to meet everyone's taste.

Sarah immediately curled up on a plush pillow chair with an iPod and earphones, which she clamped to her head, shutting everyone else out. Martin went over to the bookcase and studied the video game titles.

Emily was vaguely disappointed. Robbing a bank—it seemed so . . . so ordinary. It was a felony, of course, but she'd been expecting something *bigger*.

People didn't normally try to use her gift, which was a good thing. She hated the thought of someone trying to manipulate her. Tracey had asked her for a weather prediction once, when her family was planning a beach vacation. That wasn't a big deal. But once a crazy student teacher had demanded that she predict the week's winning lottery number. That had been seriously creepy. She'd refused to do it, but the teacher had hypnotized her and tried to force the prediction out of her.

But how could her gift provide any assistance in this plan? Would they want her to predict how much money would be in a bank's vault on a particular day? She'd never been very good at math.

"Any criminal can rob a bank," she murmured to Tracey. "What do they need *us* for?"

"To make it easier, maybe," Tracey suggested. But she admitted she was puzzled by the goal. "I thought their project would be something grander."

Martin was surprised, too. Clutching a video game box, he joined them. "I don't want to rob banks," he complained.

"Neither do we," Tracey assured him.

"I'd rather do something like *this*." Martin showed them the video game cover.

Emily read the title. "*Toxic Teen Avengers*. What is it?"

"It's a video game about these kids with super-powers who save the world."

"Save the world from what?" Tracey wanted to know. She took the box and began reading the description.

"From some other kids with superpowers who want to destroy the world," Martin replied.

Emily couldn't help smiling. "Whose side are you on, Martin? The savers or the destroyers?"

"Who cares? I just think this sounds a lot more interesting than robbing banks. And we've got superpowers, too. We could be like these guys."

Tracey shook her head. "I think a lot depends on the kind of superpowers a person has, Martin. We're not fire starters, we can't fly . . ."

"Sarah's gift is better than those powers," Martin said.

"But Sarah won't use her gift," Emily reminded him. Still, in the back of her mind, she was a little comforted to know that Sarah was capable of doing amazing things. She turned to Tracey. "Don't you think if one of us was in serious danger, Sarah would call on her powers to help out?"

"I hope she would," Tracey began, but she couldn't continue. From across the room, Sarah let out a wail.

"Sarah, are you okay?" Emily asked anxiously.

Sarah didn't hear her—she was still wearing the headset. But she was staring at her hands with horror. Emily and Tracey hurried over to her.

"What's wrong?" Tracey asked.

Sarah took the headset off. "Look at my nails," she moaned.

Emily looked, but Sarah's fingernails looked perfectly normal to her. "What's wrong with them?"

"They're all bitten! I don't bite my nails!"

"You're nervous," Tracey said, trying to comfort her. "We all are. You probably didn't even realize you were biting them."

It seemed odd to Emily that Sarah would be agonizing over her fingernails when they were all being held captive. She'd never struck Emily as being particularly vain, but of course, she didn't know her all that well.

"Maybe that woman Clare has a nail file," she suggested, but now Sarah was looking beyond her, and her eyes were wide with fear.

"Where's Carter?" she asked in a whisper.

Emily and Tracey looked around the room. Carter was so quiet and unobtrusive that people frequently didn't even notice if he was around. But he was definitely not in the room.

"In the bathroom?" Tracey suggested.

"I think he's gone," Sarah said.

"Gone where?" Emily asked.

Now Sarah was trembling. "I think . . . when you told them he doesn't have a gift . . . they just got rid of him. I mean, if he can't help them rob banks, what good is he?"

"You think they sent him back to Meadowbrook?" Emily wondered.

"I think they killed him." Sarah choked on the words, and her eyes filled with tears. Tracey sat down on the puffy chair and put an arm around her.

"Calm down," she said soothingly. "Those people didn't seem like killers to me. I'm sure Carter's all right."

Sarah pushed Tracey's arm away. "I don't care what they did to Carter. I'm worried about *me*!"

"Sarah!" Emily exclaimed.

"Shh," Sarah hissed and beckoned the two girls closer. She glanced over at Martin to make sure he wasn't listening, and then she spoke in a whisper. "I'm not Sarah."

For a moment, both Tracey and Emily were silent. Then they looked at each other, and Emily was pretty sure they were both drawing the same conclusion. The girl's next words confirmed it.

"I'm Amanda."

A small groan escaped Emily's lips, and she could

have sworn she heard Tracey mutter something stronger.

"What else could I do?" Amanda demanded. She glared at Emily. "It's all your fault, you know. You told me I'd be the next one to disappear, and I believed you. That's why I took over Sarah's body."

"Wait a minute," Tracey interjected. "I thought you could only do that if you felt sorry for the person."

Amanda nodded. "That's right."

"How could you feel sorry for Sarah?" Emily wanted to know. "She's smart, she's cute, she's not a nerd or anything like that."

"She's got really big feet," Amanda said. "And she doesn't have a boyfriend."

"That's all you needed to feel sorry for her?" Tracey asked. "Big feet and no boyfriend?"

Amanda nodded. "Yeah, that's kind of weird, huh? I guess my gift is getting stronger. Or maybe it's just easier for me to feel sorry for anyone who's not me."

Tracey and Emily exchanged looks again. "Amanda, this is not good news," Tracey said sternly.

"We were counting on Sarah's gifts to get us out of here."

"She never uses them anyway," Amanda pointed out.

"Yeah, but we figured if we got into a bad situation, she'd give in and help us out," Emily told her. She looked at Amanda thoughtfully. "You don't have Sarah's gifts by any chance, do you?"

Amanda shook her head. "I tested myself at breakfast. I tried to make you spill your juice."

"Thanks a lot," Emily muttered.

"Well, like I said, it's your fault I'm here. And it's not like I can just snap my fingers and get back into myself—you know it's not that easy. It's harder getting out than getting in." She looked at Tracey accusingly. "Do you think I would have stayed in your body for so long if I could have gotten out faster?" She got up and began to pace. "You know what really bugs me? That I believed you! Everyone knows your predictions are off the wall most of the time. If I'd just stayed myself, I would have been fine."

Emily wasn't even aware she was smiling until Amanda asked, "What's so funny?"

"It was Sarah I saw disappearing. I only said it was you because you were getting on my nerves and I wanted to scare you."

Amanda scowled. "So it's even more your fault than I thought. And when the kidnappers find out I don't have any talent, they'll get rid of me just like they got rid of Carter."

Emily had a feeling an apology would be appropriate at that moment, but she didn't think it would make Amanda feel any better. And Amanda was being so—so Amanda-ish that she didn't feel very sorry.

Tracey spoke. "Amanda, when you took over my body, after a while we started to bond or something." Amanda-Sarah looked horrified, so Tracey quickly amended that. "Okay, not like friends, but you picked up on what I could do. And you were able to disappear, remember? So maybe the same thing will happen to you now, and you'll get Sarah's powers." She turned to Emily. "Can you see if that's going to happen?"

"I'll try," Emily said. She backed away from the two girls, half-closed her eyes and let everything go blurry. Then she concentrated on a mental picture of Amanda. Slowly, the picture took on a life of its own, and she saw Amanda-Sarah in a big space where there were desks, a counter, people waiting in a line—could it be a bank? Yes, and Emily herself was there, and Tracey, too, and other people she couldn't see very well. The person who looked like Sarah was flapping her hands worriedly and looking totally useless. Frightened, too.

Then, it was like a curtain dropped briefly over the vision. When it went back up and she could see the vision again, the Sarah figure was in a completely different role. She was in control, making people move, taking charge. She looked confident, like someone with power . . .

The picture faded, and she opened her eyes. Amanda-Sarah and Tracey looked at her expectantly. "Well?" Amanda asked. "Do I get Sarah's gift?"

"I don't know," Emily said helplessly. "I had two completely different visions. In one of them you had power, and in the other one you didn't."

Tracey's eyes widened. "You saw two different futures?"

"I guess," Emily said. "And I don't know which one is right. That's never happened to me before."

"You really are worthless," Amanda declared in disgust.

"Amanda, that's not true," Tracey snapped. "Emily just happens to have a gift that's more complicated than ours."

Amanda's eyes narrowed. "I hope it's not too complicated for our kidnappers. Or she'll end up just like Carter." She gulped. "And me." Her eyes filled with fear again.

"Calm down," Tracey ordered. "We're all in this together, and we're all gifted, and we'll work together to figure this out." But this time, she didn't sound very sure of herself. Amanda certainly didn't look convinced.

"You disappeared yesterday and it didn't help us out," she said. "Martin can't turn his strength on by himself—something has to happen to him. I can't do anything as Sarah. And Emily . . . well, we just saw how useful she's going to be."

Tracey didn't have a comeback for her, and Emily didn't either. At that moment, she was experiencing something she could never have predicted.

She was in complete agreement with Amanda.

CHAPTER EIGHT

Jenna sat alone in the cafeteria. It was strange, in a way. Before she got to know Emily and Tracey, she'd always sat alone in the cafeteria, and it never bothered her. But maybe she wasn't as much of a loner as she thought she was. Now, she missed her friends.

She looked around for Ken, but she didn't see him. She *did* see Charles, and she was surprised to notice where he was sitting. His wheelchair was parked by one of the tables where the jocks sat. Among them were the basketball players Ken had been talking to that morning on the steps.

Poor Charles, Jenna thought. Did he really think he could break into *that* exclusive clique? But she didn't give this too much thought. She had more important things on her mind.

It wasn't time for class yet, but she decided that

being alone in an empty classroom was better than being alone in a crowded cafeteria, so she sneaked out of lunch early. She could think better without all the noise. And she needed to think, hard.

She wanted to make another attempt to contact Emily. Once before, when Emily had been trapped in a storage room, Jenna had been able to read her mind from a distance and come to her rescue. Of course, Emily hadn't been very far away that time—the room was in the basement of the school. But maybe she wasn't far away now. Or maybe Jenna's gift could extend to longer distances. In any case, it was worth the effort.

She concentrated with determination in the silence of room 209. But the effort was wasted. As hard as she tried, she couldn't hear Emily. Or Sarah, Tracey, Martin, or Carter. She slumped back in her seat and wished someone else would arrive in the classroom to distract her from her own thoughts.

Someone did—but it was only Amanda-the-robot, or whatever that thing was who looked like Amanda. The pretty duplicate went to her seat and pulled out her cosmetics case. Without much hope, Jenna tried to communicate.

"Hey, Amanda."

"Amanda" tore her eyes away from her own reflection. "What?"

"You wouldn't happen to know where the real Amanda is, would you?"

The blank expression on fake Amanda's face gave Jenna her answer.

Ken came in next, followed by Charles. Ken looked glum. Charles was beaming.

Jenna started with Ken. "What's up?"

Ken scowled and rubbed his forehead. "Someone's been bugging me."

Jenna knew what he meant. Every now and then, dead people tried to send him on a mission. Ken's problem was that he was essentially a nice guy, and he hated to say no. So he kept putting them off, telling them "not now" or "maybe later," and they kept on nagging him.

"Just put your foot down and make it clear that you're not going to run their afterlife errands for them," Jenna advised. "They'll have to give up sooner or later."

Ken shook his head. "This one's a mother. I don't think she's ever going to give up." He blinked. "What's that noise? I don't think it's coming from inside my head."

"It's Charles," Jenna told him. "He's whistling."

Charles had never whistled in class before, and they both turned to stare at him.

"That tune sounds kind of familiar," Jenna said.

"No kidding," Ken replied. "It's the school fight song. Don't you ever go to any games?"

"No."

"Hey, Charles, what's going on?" Ken asked. "Are you getting school spirit or something?"

"Just trying to remember the tune," Charles said cheerfully. "I'm going to the basketball game this afternoon."

Ken sighed. "Charles, if you're going to get into sports, why don't you back winners? Watch the wrestlers or the soccer guys. Our basketball team stinks this year."

"They won the past two games," Charles pointed out.

"Yeah, but they lost the ten games before that, and they lost big time," Ken said. "And it's only Mike Brady who's scoring."

Charles stopped smiling. "That's your opinion. I'll bet they make it to the finals this year."

Ken shook his head. "Nah, no way. A team can't get to the finals with only one good forward. Mike can't keep this up—he's not that great a player."

"So why do you go to all the games?" Charles demanded to know.

Ken shrugged. "Those guys are my buddies."

"Yeah, well, they're my buddies, too," Charles declared.

Ken rolled his eyes in disbelief.

"He was sitting with them at lunch today," Jenna told him.

Ken grinned, as if he assumed she was joking. "Yeah, right. Anyway, don't expect much from your buddies today, Charles. Who are we playing? St. Mark's? They've got an amazing team. They

114

haven't lost yet this season. I hate to say it, but our guys are doomed."

"Don't talk about my friends like that," Charles yelled.

Suddenly the big fat dictionary on Madame's desk rose and took off in the direction of Ken's head, moving fast.

"Charles!" Madame was in the doorway. "Stop that at once!"

The book froze in midair. Then, at half the speed, it sailed back to Madame's desk.

"Don't waste your gift on nonsense," Madame said as she went to her desk. "That goes for all of you. Your gifts may be needed for more important purposes."

"Like what?" Charles asked.

"Charles, have you not noticed that half the class is missing?"

"Oh, that."

Madame glared at Charles and seemed about to lecture him when the door opened. Jenna gasped when she saw Carter Street walk into the room.

"Carter!" Madame exclaimed. "Where have you been? Are you all right?"

Jenna almost laughed. Did Madame really expect a response? Carter never spoke, and today was no exception. Without making eye contact with anyone in the class, he went to his usual seat and sat down.

Madame studied him for a minute. Then she turned to Jenna.

"Jenna, read his mind. See if you can find out where he's been."

Jenna now had another reason to gasp. Madame had never asked her to read someone's mind before. In fact, she was always telling Jenna to stay out of other people's heads. She'd been scolded numerous times for invading the private thoughts of classmates.

But there was one student in the class whose mind had always been closed to her. "I've tried to read his mind before, Madame. I can't get anything."

"Try again," Madame ordered.

"Okay." She looked at the boy and concentrated. It was as she expected—nothing was revealed to her. After a moment, Madame asked, "Would it help to get closer to him?"

"Maybe," Jenna said, but without much hope. She got up and took the vacant seat in front of Carter. Moving the chair so she could face him, she stared into his eyes. Carter stared right back. She tried to think of her gift as an x-ray, something that could see through anything. And maybe she really was penetrating Carter's mind. But all she saw was complete darkness, a black void. She didn't know if he was intentionally blocking her gift or if there was just nothing there.

"I'm sorry, Madame." She started to turn away, but something about Carter's face made her look at him again. "Madame, his eyes look funny. Like, sort of watery. The way mine get when I have a cold."

Madame approached and gazed at him thoughtfully. "Yes, I see what you mean. And he's more pale than usual." She turned.

"Amanda, would you accompany Carter to the infirmary, please?"

Obviously programmed to behave like Amanda, Other-Amanda let out a heart-rending sigh. Then, with an expression of great reluctance, she got up.

"Carter, go with Amanda," Madame said. And as always, Carter obeyed a direct command.

They had just left the classroom when Ken uttered a word that was highly frowned upon by Meadowbrook teachers. It wasn't typical of him, and Madame looked more concerned than annoyed.

"Ken? What's wrong?"

He was clutching his head with both hands. Jenna didn't even have to concentrate to read his thoughts. She thought everyone might be able to hear the shouting that was going on in poor Ken's head.

You must talk to my son. It's urgent! My boy is in big trouble, and he needs my advice.

"Leave me alone!" Ken pleaded.

This is important! Listen to me. You have to contact him, now!

"No! Get out of my head!"

Jenna jumped. She'd never heard Ken sound so angry.

Jenna and Madame watched him anxiously. A few seconds passed, and Ken's eyes widened.

"Hey, I think she's gone."

"See?" Jenna said. "I told you, you just have to be tough with these dead people."

Madame, however, still looked worried. "Ken . . . you're sure you haven't heard from, from . . . " she looked like she was having trouble saying the words ". . . from the missing students?"

Ken shook his head. "No, Madame. I'd listen to one of them. I just hope . . . " his voice trailed away.

"You hope what?" Madame asked.

"I just hope I won't have to."

By the end of the school day, Jenna's frustration level had reached an all-time high. It was pathetic—working math problems, conjugating Spanish verbs, and playing volleyball in gym class when her friends were missing and possibly in grave danger. And here she was, doing nothing about it.

Her thoughts went back to Carter. He had to know something. He was their only link to the others. If she couldn't read his mind, maybe she could get some information out of him another way.

Back in the days when she'd run with a pretty rough street crowd, she'd known some scary people. At least, they knew how to act scary. Jenna could recall a few tactics that just might shake up Carter and frighten him out of his usual zombie state. The last bell had rung, and students were leaving the building, but there were a lot of afterschool activities going on—club meetings, the basketball game—so the infirmary had to stay open. There was a good chance Carter might still be there.

Unfortunately, the school nurse was still there, too. It wasn't going to be easy to threaten Carter with her watching.

"Yes?" the nurse asked. "Can I help you?"

Jenna thought rapidly. "There was an explosion in the chemistry lab! A teacher told me to come and get you."

The nurse rose from her desk and glanced into the little room off the reception area. Whatever she saw must have reassured her because she snatched up a bag and hurried out.

Jenna berated herself—she should have sent the nurse to the gym, which was all the way on the other side of the school. It wouldn't take her long to get up a flight of stairs and see that there was nobody lying on the floor of the lab. Jenna didn't have much time.

In the little room, there were four cots, but only one was occupied. Carter was sleeping.

"Carter!" Jenna said sharply. "Wake up!"

Carter didn't move. She went over to him and poked his arm. "Come on, Carter, wake up!"

There was still no response. She put her hands on both his thin arms and shook him. But the guy could really sleep. If she hadn't seen his chest going up and down, she would have thought he was dead.

But Carter was weird in so many ways. When he was awake, he was like a sleepwalker. It made sense that his actual sleep would be something else altogether.

Now what was she going to do? The nurse would be back any minute. Another idea occurred to her. If Carter was in a really deep sleep, he could be dreaming—and there was a chance he could be dreaming about his recent experiences. And if he was really, truly unconscious, maybe he wouldn't be able to block her efforts to read his mind.

Having never tried to read the mind of a sleeping person, she wasn't sure if it would work. But it turned out to be even easier than reading a mind that was completely awake and alert. She didn't even have to concentrate very hard—an image formed almost immediately.

It was a house—a large house that looked old and abandoned. Windows were boarded up, and a door that had once been red was covered with graffiti. There was something vaguely familiar about the scene.

"Excuse me, young lady!" A very irate nurse stood in the doorway with her hands on her hips. "What's going on? There was no explosion upstairs! And what are you doing in here with my patient?"

"Gosh, I thought I heard something. It must have been my imagination. Sorry!" Jenna slipped past the nurse and scurried out of the infirmary.

She had to share this news with someone who would care. First she ran up to room 209, but Madame wasn't there. Then she remembered Charles talking about the basketball game. Had Ken said he was going, too?

Outside the gym, she could hear yelling and cheering. When she pushed the door open, it was practically deafening. *How could people get so excited about a stupid basketball game?* she wondered. Especially since, according to Ken, Meadowbrook's team wasn't so great.

Not according to the scoreboard though. Under the heading "Home," the number was 110. Under "Visitors," the score read 0. Jenna vaguely recalled Ken saying they were playing some superduper team today. It certainly didn't look that way to her.

But Jenna wasn't really interested, and she didn't waste any more time thinking about the score. She scanned the bleachers for Ken. Finally she spotted him, way up on the top level.

"Excuse me, sorry, excuse me," she chanted while squeezing by the cheering fans. When she reached the top, she practically pushed some guy off the stands in order to plant herself down next to Ken.

Ken glanced at her, but his eyes went back to the game immediately. "Can you believe this?" he exclaimed. "I don't know what happened to these guys, but they're playing brilliantly! It's not just Mike—they're all making baskets. And St. Mark's can't even score! They can't even get the ball near the net."

"Who cares?" Jenna asked impatiently. "Ken, listen, I read Carter's mind!"

That tore his attention away from the court. "What did you find out?"

"Just the image of a house. But that could be where he was being held, and where the others are now."

"Where's the house?"

"I don't know," Jenna admitted. "But I've got this feeling I've seen it before. I just need to remember . . ."

"Oh, forget about it!"

Jenna was taken aback by Ken's reaction. Then she realized that he wasn't responding to her—his eyes had strayed back to the basketball court. A boy, one of the guys Ken knew, stood at one end of the court and held a ball. He was looking at the hoop at the other end of the court.

"I can't believe Mike's going to try that," Ken said. "Why doesn't he toss it to another player? There's no way he can make a basket from that distance."

Looking at Mike's position on the court, Jenna had to agree. She knew nothing about basketball, but she couldn't imagine any normal person being able to throw a ball that far and actually meet a target. Then she realized that something far from normal was going on.

"Ken, look!" She pointed at Charles, whose wheelchair was parked at the bottom of the opposite bleachers. He was staring at the basketball with an expression that was very familiar. And when the ball left the hands of the player, it flew the length of the court and fell right into the basket, so neatly that the net didn't even rustle.

A roar went up from the crowd. But even with all the noise, Jenna didn't miss the groan that came from Ken.

"I can't believe it!" He smacked the side of his head. "Charles is moving the ball for them!"

"Do you think the team knows he's doing it?" Jenna wondered.

"I doubt it," Ken said. "They don't know about his gift—nobody at school does, except for us." Then he frowned. "But Mike was asking me about him earlier. He called Charles spooky."

Spooky . . . The word ignited something deep in her memory. Back when she was hanging with the low-life types and staying out all night, they were always looking for shelters when the weather was bad.

She drew in her breath so sharply that Ken looked at her in alarm. "Are you okay?"

"I just remembered," she said. "I know where that house is."

CHAPTER NINE

E ARLIER THAT SAME afternoon, Emily
sat with Amanda-Sarah on a sofa facing the
big flat-screen TV. Amanda had chosen the
DVD they were watching, a romantic comedy. It
didn't matter to Emily, though, since she wasn't
actually watching it. She was more interested in
trying to drum up a vision.

More than ever before, she needed to see the
future. She had to know what they were about to
face so they could prepare themselves—to fight? To
escape? How could she help them if she didn't know
what was in store for them?

It was easy to zone out in front of the movie
because she'd already seen it and hadn't really
enjoyed the first time. Amanda was totally engrossed
in it and wouldn't interrupt her. Martin was playing
a video game—either saving or destroying the

world—and the last time she'd looked, Tracey had been reading. She was in a decent environment for receiving visions.

And the visions came, one after another. The only problem was, they didn't make any sense to her. She saw Martin lifting the very sofa she was sitting on and leaning back to throw it across the room. She saw Tracey disappearing and reappearing, blinking on and off like a light on a Christmas tree. She saw Charles breaking down a door with his mind . . . Wait a minute. Charles? He wasn't even here! Maybe someday, somewhere, Charles might break down a door, but what did that have to do with their own immediate future? It wasn't like he'd break down *this* door to rescue them—Charles wouldn't lift a finger to help anyone but himself.

Frustrated, she shook her head violently in the hope that this might clear her mind. What was it Madame had said about her visions? She had to interpret, to look for clues that would give the visions meaning.

If Martin threw the sofa really hard, and if he threw it at the door, there was a good chance the sofa would break it down. Then they could get out. Even if only one of them made it through, that one person could get help for them all. But would Martin throw the sofa toward the door? She needed to conjure up the vision again and see exactly where the sofa would go. She could be standing by the door when Martin lifted the sofa, ready to escape and run for help. Or maybe Tracey should be there instead. She could disappear—and be much harder to catch if Clare and the others went after her as she ran away.

She looked over to where she'd last seen Tracey. They needed to talk about this and get a plan organized.

Tracey wasn't there.

Emily went over to Martin, who was still playing his *Toxic Teen Avengers* video game.

"Where did Tracey go?"

Martin didn't take his eyes off the screen. "I don't know."

"Did you see her leave the room?"

"No. Whoa, did you see that? We just destroyed France!"

"Congratulations," Emily murmured.

Martin turned to her. "Hey, you know what? It's not so bad here. My mother won't let me play violent games like this. The food's better here, too, and there's lots to do. And the people aren't mean."

"Not *yet*," Emily said. "I'm going to look for Tracey."

But Tracey wasn't in the bathroom or the bedroom. Had she gone invisible to do some snooping? Emily went back to the living room.

"Tracey?" she called softly.

To her relief, Tracey suddenly reappeared. "I was looking around," she began, and then stopped. From behind her, Emily could hear the sound of someone clapping. She turned to see Clare standing there.

At least, she *thought* it was Clare. This time, the woman had her hair in a short black bob, and she was wearing a sharp business suit. Only the pale blue eyes and the hard voice assured her that this was really the same woman. It was impossible to guess what she really looked like, Emily realized.

"Very good, Tracey," Clare said. "I'm pleased

to see how well your gift works. I'd like to see demonstrations from all of you."

As soon as she left the room, Amanda-Sarah hurried over to Tracey and Jenna. "What am I going to do?" she asked in a panic.

A germ of a notion popped into Emily's head. "I've got an idea." She glanced at Martin to make sure he was still absorbed in his game. From the way he'd been talking earlier, she wasn't sure he should be included in any plans to foil the kidnappers.

They were called in for an afternoon snack a few minutes later and presented with a make-your-own-sandwich buffet.

"Wow, this is great," Martin enthused as he spread huge gobs of peanut butter on a slice of bread. "My mother never gives me peanut butter."

Emily wasn't very hungry, but she forced herself to eat. She knew she had to keep up her energy levels.

Clare and the two men ate with them, so the girls were on edge. Fortunately, the adults seemed most interested in talking with Martin, and Martin was happy to answer their questions.

"Does your gift cause you problems at school, Martin?" Clare asked.

"Oh sure," Martin said. "People don't believe how strong I am. But if they mess with me, they're in for a big surprise. Once the captain of the wrestling team picked on me. He ended up out cold."

Emily remembered that. An ambulance had to be called, and the big guy was carried out of school on a stretcher.

"You must have gotten into some serious trouble," Howard commented.

Martin grinned and shook his head. "Nope. When the guy accused me of attacking him, nobody believed him!"

"So people don't know about your gift?" George asked.

"Some people know about it because they've seen me in action," Martin said. "But then later, they look at me and they think, No way he did so much damage. Once I hit someone so hard, he went out a window on the second floor. Luckily for him, he landed in a bush, or he could have had serious injuries. A couple other kids were witnesses. But when the teacher asked them about it, they said the boy fell."

"Because they were afraid of you?" Clare wanted to know.

"Probably," Martin said proudly.

Emily doubted that. It was more likely that the kids didn't believe their own eyes. Who would believe someone as babyish and whiny as Martin could have that kind of power?

"I'll bet bigger guys are always challenging you," Howard commented.

"Oh sure, all the time," Martin said. "Everyone wants to fight the champ, right?"

Amanda-Sarah started coughing loudly, and Tracey looked down at her plate. Emily was positive they were trying very hard to keep from laughing out loud, just like her.

She had to wonder why Martin wasn't more nervous about having to demonstrate his gift to Clare and the men. Had he managed to convince himself that he was in control of his strength? That he could turn it on and off at will? In her opinion, he was going to have more problems than the fake Sarah. He didn't even have Emily and Tracey helping him out.

Control . . . Did these kidnappers have any idea how hard it was for the so-called gifted class to use their gifts effectively? Tracey was making progress, but she still had to use her memory, and sometimes her mood just wouldn't let her disappear. Jenna could be blocked by strong people who knew about her gift and had worked up enough power to protect their thoughts. Amanda had to feel pity before she could take over someone's body.

Emily wasn't sure if Ken could call on a dead person or if he had to wait until someone contacted him. Martin had to be bullied and teased before his strength emerged. And Sarah refused to use her gift at all.

As far as she could tell, Charles was the only one in the class who had complete control of his gift—which made her wonder why *he* hadn't been brought here. It seemed to her that he had the best gift for robbing banks—he could probably make all the money fly out of the bank and into the criminals' hands. And he'd be just as willing to get involved as Martin was—neither of them had any sense of loyalty.

She was pondering this question when Clare spoke to her. "Emily? Are you having a vision?"

"No," Emily replied. "I was just . . . you know, thinking."

George looked interested. "But isn't that how you see the future? By just thinking about it?"

Emily squirmed uncomfortably. "Sort of, I guess. But not really."

"Then how does it happen?" Clare demanded.

"I—I don't know."

"Personally," Howard said, "I don't care how she does it, I just want to see her do it."

"Yes," Clare said. "I told you all we wanted to see demonstrations of your gifts. Let's start now." The frosty eyes were on Emily. "With you."

Emily swallowed what felt like a peach stone in her throat. "Now? Here?"

"Yes. I want you to tell us the future of our project."

Emily took a deep breath. She looked at Tracey, and then at Amanda-Sarah, and hoped they'd remember what they hadn't had time to practice. It was mainly up to her, though, and for Amanda's sake, she had to pull it off.

"No."

Clare frowned. "What?"

"No, I won't do it. I won't try to see the future, and you can't make me."

Martin stared at her as if she were nuts. "Of course they can! They're in charge, dummy. Haven't you ever heard of torture?"

For a moment, Emily thought the snack she'd just eaten was going to come right back up. Her eyes darted between pretty, glamorous Clare; Howard who looked like a teddy bear; and serious, bespectacled George, who reminded her of a math teacher. Looks could be very deceiving.

Tracey piped up. "They don't have to torture Emily to get information, Martin. They can use Sarah to get it out of her."

Clare's eyebrows shot up. "Is this true, Sarah? I know that you're capable of making people move. Can you make them think and speak, too?"

For a moment, Sarah's face was blank, like she was

totally bewildered by the conversation. Emily and Tracey both looked at her, and her expression cleared.

"Yeah, sure. I can make Emily do anything. You want to see her act like a duck?"

"No, that won't be necessary. Just make her see the future of our project and tell us about it."

"Okay," Amanda-Sarah said. Looking at Emily and speaking in a very low voice, she growled, "Listen very carefully. You will do as I say."

If she hadn't been playing a role herself, Emily would have burst out laughing. Amanda sounded like an amateur magician in a school talent show. Somehow Emily managed to keep a straight face and stare right back at her.

"We want to know what's going to happen when we rob the bank."

Martin broke in. "That's *banks*, plural. Right? We're going to rob a lot of banks."

"That's right, Martin," Clare said, and Emily could almost detect a hint of approval in those steely eyes. "But we'll be satisfied if we can just learn what's going to happen on the first mission."

Emily acted the way she would if she was truly trying to have a vision. She let her eyelids drop lightly to make her surroundings go hazy, and she tuned out all sounds.

A few seconds later, she began to speak. "I see a big room. It's—it's a bank. The Northwest National Savings and Loan Association. There's a long counter, and a few people are standing in line waiting to see the people who work there. Behind the counter, there's a locked door that leads down a corridor and into a vault. Tracey . . . Tracey's invisible. She follows a banker through the door to the vault when he unlocks it."

Clare spoke. "Tell us what Sarah is doing, Emily."

"She's . . . she's doing something so people can't move. I think. It's hard to see her. She's blurry."

"What does Martin do?"

"He breaks down the door. Behind the door, there's a safe."

"Do you know the combination of the safe, Emily?" Clare asked.

"No, I can't see it. But the banker has gone into the vault to open the safe, so Tracey will see the combination. There's a lot of money in the safe. You're waiting for Tracey, Sarah, and Martin outside in an SUV. You drive away."

"So the robbery is a success," Clare said.

"Yes," Emily replied.

"Thank you, Emily." Clare permitted herself a frosty smile. "Well, we've now seen what Tracey, Sarah, and Emily can do. That just leaves Martin. But we're not going to ask Martin to demonstrate his gift right now. We've been told by a trusted eyewitness about the havoc Martin can create, and we don't want any broken dishes. We'll think of a way he can show us his talents later. Now, you're all free to do as you please this afternoon."

"Can we leave?" Tracey asked.

Clare gave her a chilly look. "No."

Back in the living room, Martin returned to his video game. Amanda-Sarah and Tracey gathered with Emily.

"I think we pulled that off pretty well," Tracey declared.

"Oh, absolutely. We totally fooled them," Amanda-Sarah agreed.

"Not because of you," Tracey stated. "Where did you come up with that silly hypnosis voice?"

"It wasn't silly!" Amanda protested.

Tracey turned to Emily. "How did you keep from laughing?"

Emily shrugged. "I don't know."

"And that was a great story you gave them," Tracey added. "It sounded totally believable, like you were really seeing the future."

Emily tried to smile. "Thanks."

Amanda was still annoyed over Tracey's criticism of her performance. "I think I was very believable. I sounded just like Sarah."

"How would you know what Sarah sounds like?" Tracey asked. "I'll bet you've never had a single conversation with her in your whole life."

While the two of them bickered, Emily crept away. She took a book from the bookshelf without even looking at the title. Then she sat down, opened it, and stared at a page without reading a word. Maybe if she looked like she was engrossed in the book, the others wouldn't bother her. She couldn't let them get too close—they might be able to see how upset she really was.

There was a reason why she'd been able to make her story of the future sound so real. She hadn't made anything up—she wasn't that creative.

It was a very precise and realistic vision—the clearest, most detailed vision she'd ever had. It didn't require any interpretation. It was a real vision of a very real crime. What she'd just told them was exactly what would happen.

Chapter Ten

"I t was about three months ago," Jenna told Ken. She had to yell into his ear to be heard, since the crowd was still cheering that last unbelievable basket. "I was with these friends." She hesitated. Just about everyone knew about her reputation, but she didn't want Ken getting the wrong idea about her.

"Well, they weren't exactly friends, just some people I was hanging out with because I had some problems at home, and—"

"Yeah, okay, whatever," Ken said impatiently. "What about the house?"

"We were looking for a place to sleep for the night," she confessed. "We'd been kicked out of the bus station . . ." She paused again. Thinking about her past on the streets wasn't easy. "Anyway, we saw this abandoned house, and we tried to find a way in, but it was all boarded up. I was kind of glad because the house looked so spooky to me. One of the guys, he had a can of paint, and he started spraying graffiti on the door. I don't know why. That was the house I saw in Carter's mind."

"Do you remember where it is?"

"I think so. I'll bet that's where Tracey and the rest of them are."

"There's only one way to find out for sure," Ken said. He stood up. "Is it far? Can we get there by walking?"

Jenna rose, too. "Shouldn't we go to the police and tell them?"

"Tell them what? That you read Carter's mind and now you know where the missing kids are? Come on, Jenna. They're not going to buy that."

He was right—Jenna knew that. There was also the fact that certain police officers might recognize her . . . and they would be even less likely to believe any story she might tell them.

"But even if we find the house, what can we do?" she asked Ken. "Break in and rescue them? Whoever kidnapped them must be there, too, watching them. Maybe with weapons. How can we fight them?"

Ken thought for a minute. "We need Charles," he said finally. "Even if the kidnapper has a gun, Charles could get it out of his hand. Come on, let's get him."

At that moment, a whistle blew and a huge roar went up from the fans. Jenna glanced at the scoreboard and saw that Meadowbrook had won by a landslide.

They pushed through the excited crowd and made their way to the gym floor. Charles was still in the same place, applauding wildly and watching the team congratulate each other, slapping hands in the air and clapping each other on the back. Ken and Jenna hurried to his side.

"We think we know where the missing kids are," Ken told him hurriedly. "You have to come with us."

Charles stopped clapping. "Why?"

"Because you can make things move!" Jenna said in exasperation. "You might have to make a gun drop out of someone's hand or make a door open."

"I can't," Charles said. "Mike and the guys are going out for pizza and they invited me to come."

He smiled happily. "They think I bring them good luck."

"Oh for crying out loud!" Ken exclaimed. "Charles, your classmates could be in big trouble! Don't you want to save them?"

"I'd rather go out for pizza with the basketball team," Charles replied.

"Too bad," Ken growled. He went behind Charles and grabbed the handles of his wheelchair. Charles pushed on the brake so the chair couldn't roll.

One of the players saw them. "Hey, what do you think you're doing? Leave Charles alone!" He started to come toward them, and several teammates joined him. They didn't look happy.

"Ken, we can't force him to come with us," Jenna said hurriedly. "And I think we'd better get out of here or we won't be going anywhere either."

Once outside the gym, Ken turned to Jenna. "Which way?"

"You know the industrial park behind the bus station? It's just past that."

Across the street, in front of the mall, they had to wait almost half an hour for a bus, which let them off in front of the bus station twenty minutes later. It took them another fifteen minutes to make their way through the industrial park. But the house was right where Jenna remembered it was.

Without speaking, she and Ken went to the front of the place and looked for an entrance. She recognized the graffiti on the red door. Without much optimism, she gave it a push, but it didn't budge. They wandered around and looked for another way to get in. But the house was so boarded up, they couldn't even make out if there was a light on inside. They couldn't hear anything either.

Ken pressed his face up against a crack in a board. Seconds later he let out a cry of pain.

"What?" Jenna cried out in alarm.

"It's that woman in my head again!" Ken moaned.

Jenna could hear her. *Talk to my son! Give him a message from me! It's important!*

"Get out, get out!" Ken yelled.

"Shh," Jenna hissed. "I'll go and check out the other side of the house."

She didn't expect to find anything there that might give her a clue as to whether anyone was inside, but she needed to get away from Ken and what was going on in his head. She had an idea.

She thought about the time she'd been able to hear Emily's call for help. If Emily *was* in this house, Jenna was closer to her than she'd been that time. She pressed the side of her head against the house and concentrated.

She heard nothing—not through her ears, not through her head. She knew Emily was capable of blocking Jenna's mind-reading skills, but surely at a time like this she'd be trying to make contact.

She thought she heard something—a dull, low murmur. It could have been the wind in the nearby trees, she supposed. Or maybe her own heartbeat. But somehow, at that moment, she knew for certain that Emily was in this house. The others, too, probably, and whoever was holding them captive. But it was Emily she sensed. Emily was close by, maybe even leaning against this very same wall on the other side. If only she could understand what Emily was thinking. She was a mind reader, so why couldn't she read the mind behind this wall?

Because the mind on the other side of the wall

wasn't sending a message. It was showing her a mood. Jenna could feel it. It was like a thick, dark cloud coming down over her, enveloping her in despair. Sadness. Hopelessness. That was what Emily was feeling at that minute.

Ken joined her. "I got rid of that woman. Have you seen anything?"

"Emily's in big trouble," Jenna told him. "Which means they all are. We have to get in there, Ken."

Ken nodded grimly. "Which means we have to get Charles."

CHAPTER ELEVEN

H EY, CHECK THIS OUT! Emily, come over here!"

Emily looked up from the book she wasn't reading. Amanda-Sarah beckoned to her. Listlessly, she rose and went to the sofa where Amanda-Sarah and Tracey were sitting.

"What?"

Amanda-Sarah's eyes were bright. "Watch this." She looked at Martin, who was in front of the screen by the Xbox console, holding the controller. His thumbs moved rapidly, hitting the buttons that controlled the action of the characters on the screen. Suddenly, he let out a yelp.

"Hey! That's not what you're supposed to do!"

Emily shrugged. "Martin's talking to the TV. So what?"

"No, you don't get it," Tracey said excitedly.

"Sarah—Amanda—whoever she is, she made Martin hit the wrong button! She's getting Sarah's gift!"

"So far, I can only make his thumbs move," Amanda-Sarah said. "But I could get stronger, I think."

"That's nice," Emily murmured.

"*Nice?* Emily, don't you see what this means? If she keeps practicing, maybe she can end this crazy business!"

Emily shook her head. "I don't think so."

"You don't think I'm going to get any better?" Amanda-Sarah asked.

"I didn't say that. You'll probably get better at using Sarah's gift, but it's not going to stop the robberies."

"Why not?" Tracey asked.

"Because . . . I just don't think it can."

Amanda-Sarah looked annoyed. "You know, you're being a real downer, Emily."

Tracey agreed. "Yeah, what's wrong with you? You act like you've given up."

Emily raised her head. What was the point of

hiding the truth anymore? They might as well know why she was so depressed.

"That story I told at lunch—it wasn't a made-up story. It was my real vision. We're going to be robbing banks."

Neither Tracey nor Amanda-Sarah responded immediately. They both stared at her like she'd lost her mind.

"I don't know why, but for some reason, we're all going to help them. When I had the vision, I didn't understand how this could happen because Amanda can't do what Sarah can do. But now that Amanda's getting Sarah's gift . . . well, it all makes sense."

They still didn't look convinced, so Emily went over the vision again.

"Remember what I said? Tracey would disappear and follow a banker into the vault, where she'd see the combination to the safe. Martin would break down the door leading to the vault. Amanda would stop the security guards from interfering. And Clare would drive everyone away in an SUV."

"I remember what you said," Tracey told her. "But

there was something you left out. Where are *you* when all this is going on?"

"I'm not absolutely sure," Emily said. "I wasn't in my own vision. Maybe I'm being held hostage. That could explain why the rest of you go along with the robbery—because they'll hurt me if you don't."

Amanda-Sarah looked skeptical. "But you're just guessing, aren't you? You didn't see yourself as a hostage in your vision."

"That's right," Tracey said. "Maybe you're not in the vision because you escaped."

Emily drew in her breath as a tiny bell rang in the back of her memory. "I forgot about that!" She sat down between the two girls. "I had another vision just before lunch. It was a vision of Martin throwing this sofa across the room with so much force that it broke the door down."

"And we escape through it?" Tracey asked excitedly.

Emily tried to remember. "That wasn't part of the vision. But somebody should be able to get out the door, shouldn't they?"

"There you are!" Tracey declared triumphantly.

"You escape, and you run for help. The rest of us go through with the robbery, but when Clare takes off in the SUV with us and the money, there's a roadblock and a dozen police cars to stop the car at the corner!"

Amanda-Sarah looked at her in surprise. "Are you having visions now, too?"

"No, I'm just being logical. This explains everything!" She turned to Emily. "What do you think?"

Emily could actually feel the dark cloud of depression begin to lift. "You're right. Madame said I had to learn how to interpret my visions instead of just taking them literally. This is a perfect example. I had a very clear vision of a successful bank robbery, with all of us playing our parts. But none of us *wants* to commit a bank robbery."

Amanda-Sarah glanced at Martin. "I'm not so sure about him."

Tracey disagreed. "I don't think Martin really wants to be a criminal. He just thinks it would be exciting, like a video game. In the real world, he'd be scared out of his mind."

"Anyway," Emily went on, "it's all starting to

make sense now. But there's still something we have to figure out." Now she directed her attention toward Martin. "How are we going to get him to throw the sofa?"

The three of them studied the small, thin boy. Oblivious to their interest, Martin's eyes remained glued to the screen while his thumbs tapped rapidly on the controller. The girls considered various options quietly and came to an agreement.

Recalling what had happened in her vision, Emily rose from the sofa and stationed herself beside the door. Amanda-Sarah also got off the sofa and then went to the opposite end of the room, where she positioned herself just behind Martin.

Tracey, the only one remaining on the sofa, spoke. "Martin, aren't you ever going to stop playing video games?"

"I like video games," Martin said.

"Maybe someone else would like to play that game," Tracey said.

"Too bad," Martin said.

Amanda-Sarah moved quickly. She leaned over

Martin's shoulder and snatched the controller out of his hand.

"Hey!" Martin cried in outrage.

"Too bad for *you*, Martin," Amanda-Sarah sang.

Martin jumped up. Amanda-Sarah held the controller high over her head. Martin, who came up only as far as her shoulders, hopped up and down, trying to get it.

Amanda-Sarah laughed. "Give up, Martin. You'll never be tall enough to reach this.

"Give it back!" Martin yelled.

"Does itty-bitty Martin want his toy?" Amanda-Sarah said. "Maybe Emily will give it to you." She tossed the controller across the room, and Emily caught it.

It wasn't as easy for her to tease and ridicule Martin—she just didn't have Amanda's natural gift for meanness. But she did her best.

"Come and get it, Martin, if you can." She waved the controller in the air. "What's the matter? Are you scared of me?"

Martin ran over to her. When he was within a

foot of reaching her, she threw the device back to Amanda-Sarah.

Once again, Amanda-Sarah taunted him by holding it too high. By now, Martin was shrieking, and his face was red.

"Here, Martin," Amanda-Sarah said, extending the controller in his direction. But as he reached out for it, she threw it to Tracey on the sofa.

Tracey held the controller. "Martin, I'm not moving. You can come right over here and take it out of my hand."

Martin raced over to the sofa. But just as he reached Tracey, she disappeared. And since she was holding the controller, it vanished along with her.

"Come back!" Martin screamed.

She did. He reached. She disappeared again.

Emily recalled her vision of Tracey blinking on and off like a Christmas tree light. And here it was, happening in real life—another accurate vision!

Martin's screams were louder now, and Emily wasn't surprised to see George and Clare run into the living room. She was a little worried though. Would she be able to get out the door before they came after her? Could Tracey and Amanda-Sarah block them to give her some extra time?

Martin was completely frustrated now. He'd been teased to his limit, and he responded just as the girls had assumed he would. In a rage, he grabbed one end of the sofa and lifted it. He raised the large piece of furniture in the air over his head and leaned back as if to give himself the momentum to throw it. Emily tensed up and prepared herself to move. And then . . .

Martin let out a high-pitched squeal. So did Amanda-Sarah. And Emily saw why. A little gray mouse raced across the baseboard and disappeared into a little hole. It must have startled Martin so deeply that he forgot about being teased.

Which meant he lost his superstrength. The sofa dropped to the ground with a thud. There was no open door for Emily to run through. She'd screwed up the vision again.

At least Clare and George were impressed. "Martin, you *are* strong!" Claire exclaimed.

Once again the woman had changed her look. Now she looked like she could be a celebrity, a singer or an actress. Her hair was blond again, but this time it was long and *big*, all curls, very glamorous. Dangling gems hung from her ears and she wore a tight, sparkly red dress and stiletto heels. Amanda-Sarah gasped.

"Ooh, you look *hot!*" she exclaimed.

It was hard to read any expression in those transparent eyes, but Emily could have sworn the woman was pleased. "Do you think so?" she asked.

"Absolutely!" Amanda-Sarah said. "I love that dress. In my opinion, this is definitely your best look."

Emily and Tracey exchanged looks. This was so Amanda—Clare could be pure evil, and Amanda would still be impressed by her style.

Or maybe Amanda was faking her admiration, trying to buddy up with Clare so that Clare would trust her, and then she would use that trust to help her classmates. For the zillionth time, Emily wished Jenna was there. A mind reader would be so useful—much more useful than a second-rate fortuneteller like *her*.

"Red is your color," Amanda continued, but now Clare had turned her attention back to Martin.

"Was it easy for you to lift the sofa?"

Martin looked smug. "No sweat. It wasn't even heavy. I could have tossed it across the room."

George was clearly intrigued. "And you don't have to do anything to prepare yourself? Go into a trance or chant something?"

"No," Martin said nonchalantly. "I'm just your run-of-the-mill superhero."

"Bull," Amanda-Sarah muttered. Clare heard her.

"What are you saying, Sarah?"

"He can't just snap his fingers and turn into Superman."

"*Amanda!*" Tracey hissed. "I mean, *Sarah!*"

But as usual, Amanda was too caught up in her own announcement to catch the warning.

"He's acting like he can just turn it on and off. He has to be teased first until he's ready to cry, and *then* he gets the power."

"Interesting," Clare said. "All right, I think it's about time to get started."

"We're going to rob a bank *now*?" Tracey asked in dismay.

"No, not right this minute," Clare said. "We're going to have a little rehearsal first. I assume that in the past you've all used your gifts independently, to serve your own purposes. But to my knowledge, you have never worked together as a team, combining your gifts to achieve one common goal."

"How do you know that?" Tracey asked in bewilderment. "We've never seen you before—not until we were brought here."

Clare looked at her coolly. "But we've known about you for some time now, Tracey. And we know what you've all been up to."

Emily felt sick. This could only mean one thing— there was a spy among them, in their class. Charles? That could explain why he hadn't been brought here. Maybe he was already a member of this criminal team.

Then another candidate came to mind, one that made her feel even sicker. Madame . . . *She* knew them better than anyone. The students confided in her. She knew their strengths and weaknesses. She'd always claimed to be on their side. Was it possible they'd all been fooled? Had Madame betrayed them to these people?

She had no opportunity to envision Madame's future.

"Let's begin our rehearsal," Clare said. "Howard!"

The chubby guy hurried into the room. He was rubbing his hands together in delight. "Are we going to practice now? Can I play the bank manager?"

"Yes, all right," Clare said, but Emily didn't miss the look of scorn that flashed across her face. Clearly Clare didn't have much respect for Howard. So why was he on her team?

Clare indicated the sofa. "This will serve as the bank counter. The bookcase is the bank entrance. Tracey, Martin, Sarah, go and wait in front of the bookcase. Emily, where will the security guard be standing?"

Emily just glared at her. Clare sighed.

"Sarah, make Emily tell us where the guard will be standing."

By this time, Amanda might very well be able to do that, Emily thought. *And who knows what else.*

"Okay, okay, I'll tell you. He's next to the door."

Clare eyed her keenly. "You could be lying, I suppose. Well, it doesn't matter—the guard will be in uniform. Sarah, you shouldn't have any problem identifying him. George, stand over there and be the guard. Now, Tracey, Martin, and Sarah will enter together, but Tracey will be invisible. Tracey, disappear."

"Now?" Tracey asked.

"We only have time for one rehearsal," Clare said. "We need to cover everything. Disappear."

Tracey folded her arms across her chest. "What if I don't want to?"

"Then I'll order Sarah to make you disappear."

"What if Sarah refuses?" Tracey asked.

If Clare had seemed cold before, this was nothing compared to the way she looked at Tracey right that minute. It was as if icicles were shooting out of her eyes.

"Haven't you wondered where Emily is going to be while all this is going on? She'll be waiting in the car with me. And I will be armed. Do you see where this is going?"

Emily's stomach turned over. So she'd been right. This was what her mind had refused to show her. They'd hold her hostage to ensure that the others would do what they were supposed to do.

Clearly Tracey got the message, too. She faded away. Clare spoke to the empty space where Tracey had been. "And don't even think about trying to do something now either. Your friends will suffer for it."

She turned to Martin. "Martin, go to the bank counter. If there's a line, take your place in it. Don't go to the front. You mustn't draw attention to yourself. Sarah, stand behind Martin. From there, you can see the guard *and* the tellers at the counter."

"Why do I have to be able to see the tellers?" Amanda–Sarah asked. "I thought I only had to stop the guard from reacting."

"The tellers have alarm buttons under their side of the counter," Clare told her. "They can't be given any time to press the button and alert the police. You'll need to stop them as well as stop the guard. You can do that, can't you?"

"I . . . I don't know. I've never tried doing two things at once."

"Well, that's why we're having a rehearsal—to make sure you can," Clare said. She went over to the sofa and dragged one of the small end tables behind it. "We'll call this the door to the vault. Tracey, go behind the counter and stand by it so you can follow the first person who goes through."

Even though she couldn't see her, Emily assumed that Tracey was doing as she was told. She was too good a friend to risk Emily's life.

"Now we're all in place. The first thing that has to happen is that someone goes into the vault. It could be one of the tellers or the bank manager. Howard, you do it."

Howard took some keys from his pocket, jingled them in his hand, and spoke to an imaginary companion.

"Yes, of course, Mrs. Montague, we can get your diamond necklace out of your safe-deposit box. Come with me, please." He walked slowly toward the sofa and continued talking to his pretend client. "And may I ask where you will be wearing that lovely necklace? Ah, the opera! How very nice."

Clare looked at him with undisguised contempt. "Howard, we don't have much time."

Howard quickened his pace. Behind the sofa, he twisted the key as if he was putting it into a lock.

"Get right beside him, Tracey," Clare said. "Stay with him as he goes inside."

Howard acted as if he was opening a door. He made a big show of standing aside to allow the invisible Mrs. Montague to precede him, and presumably the invisible Tracey went through, too. He walked a few more steps and then made the movements of turning a combination dial.

"Watch this carefully, Tracey," Clare said. "You have to be able to remember the numbers. Now, Howard, leave the vault. Tracey, stay where you are."

Howard obeyed, once again pretending to open the door for the lady and locking it behind her. Clare's eyes remained on the position behind the sofa.

"Tracey, show yourself," she demanded sharply.

Emily held her breath. What if Tracey had run off in search of a weapon to combat the crooks? But she'd been right to assume that Tracey wouldn't risk being disobedient. Tracey reappeared, right where she was supposed to be.

"Very good," Clare said. "Now, Martin, this is your big moment. You're at the front of the line, facing the teller. I'll play the teller." They took their positions, and Clare continued.

"We want the teller to make you angry, so you'll be strong enough to break down the locked door leading to the vault. You'll have to create the right atmosphere so she'll upset you. Do you understand me?"

It was obvious Martin didn't have a clue. "Huh?"

Clare frowned. George approached her. "Actually, considering what we just saw, it might not be a good idea to practice teasing. You don't want him breaking any doors down in *here*."

Clare considered this. "But he needs to see what he has to do."

"I'll play his part," George offered, and Clare agreed. They held a brief, whispered conversation, and then Clare turned back to Martin.

"Martin, you have to watch very carefully and remember what George says. All right, George, you're Martin. What is the first thing you say to me, the teller?"

"I'd like some money, please," George said.

"Do you have a check you want to cash?" Clare asked.

"No."

"Do you have a debit card and a PIN?"

"No."

"Do you have a checking account or savings account at this bank?"

"No."

Clare shook her head. "I'm sorry, young man. You're not eligible to withdraw money here."

"But I want some," George said. "I want a million dollars. Right now."

Now Clare produced an artificial and condescending smile. "Don't we all. But that's not how the banking system operates."

"Please can I have some money? Pretty please?"

"I'm sorry, no. Now please step aside and let me help the next customer." Looking toward Martin, she said, "This is when you start crying."

George wasn't much of an actor. "Boo hoo," he said flatly. "Boo hoo. Give me some money."

"Now, Sarah, you start teasing him."

"Get out of the way! You're holding everyone up. What kind of idiot doesn't understand how a bank works?" Amanda-Sarah scoffed.

"Will that be enough to make you get strong, Martin?" Clare asked.

Martin actually looked offended. "I can call on my superpowers whenever I want!"

Amanda-Sarah piped up. "If it's not enough, I can do more. I'm good at annoying him—I can get him to explode."

Does she have to be so cooperative? Emily thought. Knowing Amanda, she was probably just relieved Emily was going to be the hostage instead of her. Amanda didn't care about anyone but herself, but Emily never would have thought she could sink so low . . . Could Amanda be the traitor among them? There were so many possible spies. Emily hadn't thought her spirits could go any lower, but now they were plummeting to depths she'd never before experienced, and that dark cloud enveloped her completely. She didn't even need to drum up a vision to know that they were all doomed.

The rehearsal continued. George went back to playing the guard, and Martin took over his own role. He made a big production out of breaking down an imaginary door, even adding sound effects.

"Emily, you stand in for the guard," Clare ordered. "Sarah, make her unable to move."

"Sure thing," Amanda-Sarah said. She fixed a wide-eyed stare in Emily's direction.

Emily tensed up, expecting some sort of cold tingle to creep over her as her body froze up. But nothing happened. She knew she could have moved if she'd wanted to.

So Amanda hadn't absorbed any more of Sarah's powers—not yet, at least. But Emily wasn't going to point that out. She stood very still and held her breath.

Clare gave a short nod. "That will be all. We'll leave for the bank at six o'clock."

"Banks aren't open at six o'clock," Tracey said.

"Northwest National is open till seven one night a week," Clare informed her. "Which happens to be tonight. Tracey, come with me. I want to teach you some tips on memorizing numbers. If any of you are hungry, there are cookies on the dining room table."

Emily watched as the adults and her classmates went into the dining room. She wasn't hungry, and there was another reason she wanted to be alone. She could feel the tears burning behind her eyes, and she didn't want them to see her cry.

It was going to happen just as she envisioned it. Well, at least now she knew she was really capable of seeing the future. But it wasn't much comfort. In one and a half hours, she'd be forced to rob a bank, and there wasn't anything she could do about it. They wouldn't be hurt—they were much too valuable to Clare. They'd just become lifetime criminals.

Amanda-Sarah came back into the room. Hastily Emily wiped her eyes, but it wasn't necessary—the body snatcher barely glanced at her.

"Have you seen my watch? I mean, Sarah's watch. I took it off around here somewhere."

"What does it look like?"

"Old-fashioned—there are these tacky little pearls all around the face. It's bad enough having

Sarah's bitten fingernails—I don't have to wear her icky jewelry . . . Oh, here it is."

Emily watched her in amazement. "How can you act so—so casual? Aren't you upset about all this?"

Amanda-Sarah shrugged. "Oh, I'm sure I'll get back into my own body pretty soon. I won't be stuck with these people forever."

"But what about the rest of us?" Emily asked.

"Don't worry," Amanda-Sarah said. "When we're all together at the bank, I'll stop them. I didn't want to do it while we were practicing because I wasn't sure I could freeze all three of them at the same time. But once we're at the bank, I'll freeze Clare while she's in the car with you. She'll let me get close enough because she likes me. Then, once we're in the bank, I'll freeze George and Howard. See? It'll be easy."

Emily sighed. "You think you can stop Clare *and* George *and* Howard from moving?"

"I stopped you, didn't I?"

"I was faking it."

The other girl's face fell. "Oh. Well, there's a chance I'll have more of Sarah's gift by the time we get to the bank. I wouldn't count on it though. When I was Tracey, I never could stay invisible very long."

Emily dropped into a chair. In the back of her mind, she must have been clinging to the tiny hope that there was still a chance to get out of this. But it wasn't to be.

"Cheer up," Amanda-Sarah said. "Maybe we can get away at the bank. You never know what will happen."

"But I *do* know what's going to happen," Emily reminded her. "That's why I'm so depressed."

Amanda-Sarah looked thoughtful. "I don't get it. I mean, how can you ever really know exactly what's going to happen in the future? You can see what *might* happen, but you can't know for sure, can you? There's always that butterfly thing."

"What are you talking about?"

"Haven't you ever heard about the butterfly effect? I saw a movie about it. A butterfly can flap its wings in Brazil and cause an earthquake in Japan. Or something else. A typhoon, maybe."

Emily was in no mood for nonsense. "Don't be stupid."

"No, really. It's like, something really small can happen, and it has an effect that builds and builds. Like the way my parents met."

Emily sank deeper into the chair. "I really don't want to hear how your parents met, Amanda."

"No, listen, it's cool. My father was on his way to a job interview. He was early, so he took a walk through a park, and when he passed too closely by some bushes, a button on his jacket was pulled off. He didn't want to look like a slob, so he ran into the first dry cleaners he saw to see if someone could sew it back on right away, before his interview. And my mother was in there picking up some clothes. That's how they met!"

Emily wasn't impressed. "So? It's what's called a coincidence."

"But, wait, think about it. If that button hadn't fallen off, they might never have met. I wouldn't have been born. So I wouldn't have taken over Tracey's body, and she'd still be that nerdy girl she used to be. You see? Tracey's okay today because my father walked through a park. Get it?"

"Not really," Emily said. Amanda–Sarah gave up and went back into the dining room.

But even as Emily returned to her private sadness, she had to admit there might be something to what she'd just heard. Like, why hadn't her vision of Martin breaking the door down happened? Because a stupid mouse ran across the floor, and Martin turned out to be afraid of mice. If it wasn't for that mouse, the police might be here right now, freeing the kids and arresting Clare and her gang.

Then she sat up straight. That wasn't exactly right. Now that she thought about it, she remembered that her vision only included Martin throwing the sofa. She'd *hoped* it would break down the door, but that wasn't part of the vision.

Okay, maybe Amanda's story was kind of interesting. Still, it didn't make her feel any better about what they were about to do. In just over an hour, they'd be robbing a bank. And she didn't see how any butterfly was going to be able to stop it from happening.

Chapter Twelve

K EN KNEW WHERE THE basketball team would be hanging out. Gino's Pizza at the mall across the street from Meadowbrook was *the* popular place for athletes. As they approached, he pointed, and Jenna saw half a dozen players squeezed into a booth by the window.

"The big question is, how are we going to get him away from his new buddies?" Jenna wondered.

Ken rolled his eyes. "Who aren't his buddies at all. Mike's superstitious—he's always been like that. He thinks Charles is some sort of good luck charm, and he's persuaded the other guys to go along with it. I mean, how else could he explain their sudden winning streak?"

"So they're totally using him," Jenna said.

"Yeah. And as soon as the season's over, they'll dump him."

"You're sure of that, huh?"

"I know these guys. I bet they make fun of Charles when he's not around."

Jenna thought about that. "Charles is proud. If he knew that they don't really like him, he'd leave."

Ken agreed. "I guess we could tell him. But he wouldn't believe us."

Jenna nodded. "But if he heard it from *them* . . ."

"What do you mean?"

An idea was forming in her head. "Do you have a cell phone?"

"Sure."

"Can I see it?"

He handed it over. Jenna had a quick look at it, grinned, and then told Ken her idea.

"It's worth a shot," he said. "Let's go." They went to the door of the restaurant.

"Wait a second," Jenna said. "How do I look?" She rearranged her features into what she hoped was a convincing expression.

"Seriously depressed," Ken said.

"On the verge of crying?"

He cocked his head to one side and scrutinized

her. "Well . . . it would be better if you could actually work up a few tears."

Jenna tried, but it was impossible. Seriously depressed would have to do.

They entered and ambled over to the table where the basketball players and Charles were sitting. "Can we squeeze in?" Ken asked. Without waiting for a reply, he pushed his friend Mike to one side and sat down next to Charles.

Charles looked at him with something that resembled interest. "I thought you were going off to save those kids from class," he muttered, too quietly for the others around the table to hear him.

"Nah," Ken replied softly. "Too much trouble. Hey, can I have a slice?"

Jenna wasn't insulted when none of the boys made room for her. She wasn't the kind of girl the jocks went for. In fact, she had a feeling she scared half of them. That made it even harder to look pathetic and win their sympathy. But she did her best.

"I'm not staying," she said in a quavering voice. She sniffed loudly and rubbed her eyes.

"What's *her* problem?" Mike asked.

"Her ring came off her finger and fell into a storm drain outside," Ken said.

"I dropped my wallet in a storm drain once," another player said. "But I got it back. I chewed some gum, put it on the end of a stick, and fished around for it. The wallet stuck to it and I pulled it out."

"We tried that," Ken said quickly. "But we couldn't find the ring."

"Tough luck," one boy said.

"Yes," Jenna said and gave a few more sniffs. "It was a very special ring. My father gave it to me before he died."

She thought that adding a sentimental touch like that might mean something to them.

One of the boys spoke. "Did you see the look on the face of that St. Mark's guy when he tried to make that shot and his ball went into the bleachers? I still can't figure that one out. I thought it would be an easy basket for him."

"Yeah, how did that happen?" another boy wondered.

"Who knows, who cares?" Mike sang out. He tossed an arm around Charles. "We've got our good luck charm. He not only helps us win, he makes the other team lose, big time!"

Jenna had to get the conversation back to her nonexistent ring. Clearly sentiment wasn't going to work. She tried another tactic.

"It had diamonds and rubies on it," she said.

The team members looked at her blankly.

"My ring," she reminded them. "The one that fell in the sewer. Diamonds and rubies. And a great big sapphire."

That impressed them.

"Real jewels?" Mike asked. "Wow, that sucks."

Ken snapped his fingers, as if a brilliant idea had suddenly occurred to him. "I know how you can get it back! Charles, could you come outside with us?"

"Why?" Charles asked.

Ken looked at him meaningfully. "You know why, Charles. We could, uh, try the stick thing again and . . . and you'd bring us luck." To the others, he added, "He's just that kind of guy, isn't he? Lucky, I mean?"

Charles glared at him. "Yeah, well, maybe I don't want to bring *you* any luck."

"Aw, c'mon Charles," Mike said. "Ken's a pal. Why don't you see if you can help his friend?"

"Yeah, maybe there's a reward in it for you," another boy said.

Jenna thought rapidly. Charles was in her math class. "I'll do your math homework for a month," she offered.

"Hey, that's a pretty good deal," one of the boys said.

Charles seemed to think so, too. "Yeah, okay." He backed his wheelchair into the aisle, and Jenna followed him out of the restaurant. Ken stayed behind at the table.

Thank goodness there really was a drain at the edge of the road just in front of the restaurant. Charles peered down into it.

"I don't see anything," he said.

"It's in there," Jenna assured him. She glanced back at the restaurant, where she could see Ken talking to the others. *C'mon, Ken, do it fast! I don't know how long I can keep him out here.*

"If it's got diamonds, I should see a sparkle," Charles said.

"The diamonds are dirty," Jenna said hurriedly. "I have to get the ring cleaned. Can't you just imagine it in your head and bring it up without seeing it?"

"I don't know. I never tried that."

"It's gold, and there's a big diamond, and a ruby on each side of the diamond, and lots of little diamonds on the band."

"I thought you said there was a sapphire."

"Oh, right. Absolutely. A humongous sapphire."

"I never saw you wear a ring like that," Charles said.

"Well, um, I'm not allowed to wear it to school. Look, just concentrate on that image, and I'll bet you can make it come out. You're so gifted, Charles—you've got the most amazing gift. You're so lucky. All I can do is read minds, but you can move things. That's so much cooler." She was jabbering now, but she'd do anything to keep

Charles out here until Ken accomplished what he had to do.

"Shut up, I'm concentrating," Charles said. A minute passed. "Nah, this isn't working. I'm going back inside."

"Just try one more time, *please!*" Jenna pleaded. "Think about all that homework you won't have to do!"

"Wait a minute," Charles said. "What kind of grades do you get in math, anyway? I don't want you doing my homework if you're going to do a bad job."

Fortunately, she didn't have to answer that. Ken came out of the restaurant.

"Did it work?" she asked excitedly.

He held up his cell phone. "I've got it right here."

"What are you guys talking about?" Charles demanded.

"Your so-called friends," Ken said. "We just thought you might like to know what they really think of you."

He turned on the phone's recording device and pressed Play. The first voice they heard was Ken's.

"So, Charles is hanging out with you now. He's really a pretty good guy when you get to know him."

A boy spoke. "Are you kidding? He's a total dweeb! That kid is too pathetic. He doesn't do anything at school—he just rolls around and complains about everything."

"He can't help being in a wheelchair." That was Ken's voice again.

"That's got nothing to do with it," another voice said. "If he wasn't in the wheelchair, he'd be a walking dweeb."

Mike spoke next. "Look, if he can get us into the finals, he can hang out with us. At least till the season's over."

"But he's really getting on my nerves," another boy said. "And we've still got a month left before the finals."

"But just think how great we'll feel when we win the state championship," a boy declared.

Mike spoke. "Not to mention how great we'll feel when we can dump Charles."

Ken turned off the phone. "I'm sorry about this, Charles. But you should know what kind of creeps you're hanging out with."

Jenna was watching Charles's face. What little color he had was gone, and it wasn't hard to see that he was really on the verge of tears. In fact, one tear was already making its way down his cheek.

"You know, Charles, we would be your friends," she said, "if you'd let us. I know Emily and Tracey would be, too." She didn't include Amanda. Charles wasn't *that* gullible. "Too bad Tracey and Emily have been kidnapped. Who knows, we may never see them again."

Fiercely, Charles brushed the tear away, but he didn't say anything. Jenna did a quick scan of his thoughts. He was on the edge.

"I mean it, Charles. I don't lie. All you've got to do is be a nice guy, and you can have all the friends you want."

There was a long moment of silence. Finally Charles spoke.

"Okay."

At that moment, a car pulled up alongside them. The driver's window came down, and a familiar voice spoke.

"Get in."

"Madame!" Jenna exclaimed. "How did you know we were here?"

Ken answered for her. "Cell phones have other functions besides recording gossip, Jenna."

The trunk of the car opened. Ken helped Charles into the front seat while Jenna folded the chair and put it in the trunk. She got into the back with Ken, and they took off.

Jenna told Madame about the house and how she sensed Emily and the others were inside. "But I could only feel her mood. I couldn't read her thoughts and find out anything specific, like why they've been taken there."

"We'll find out soon enough," Madame said grimly. She followed Jenna's directions to the old abandoned house behind the industrial park.

"Think you can get the door open, Charles?" Ken asked.

"Piece of cake," Charles replied.

As they approached the house, Jenna frowned. "Something's different."

"What?" Madame asked.

"I don't know. But I'm not feeling Emily's mood."

Madame parked the car, and they all got out. Charles rolled himself to the front of the house. He stared at the red door. Nothing happened.

"It's got chains on it," he said.

"Is that a problem?" Madame asked.

"Nah. I just have to concentrate a little harder."

His brow furrowed, and seconds later the big red door flew open—Charles had unscrewed the hinges. Ken ran toward it.

"Wait," Madame cried out. "Don't go inside. Wait for the police!"

But Ken was already inside the house. Jenna wasn't sure whether to follow him or not. It looked so dark in there.

There was something else, too. She couldn't hear any thoughts at all. With the door open, she should have been able to pick up something. It was as if there were no working brains in there at all.

Ken emerged, shaking his head. "They're gone."

"Where?" Jenna cried helplessly. But she knew no one could answer that.

Suddenly Ken put his hands to his head. "Not now!" he cried out. "Leave me alone!"

Again Jenna could hear the nagging woman's voice. *Please, talk to my son, he's going to get into trouble. You have to tell him I'm very upset with him. That will make him stop.*

"I want *you* to stop!" Ken yelled. "I don't care about your stupid son!"

He's not stupid. His name is Howard. He's really a good boy—he just got involved with bad people. I've been watching him. They've kidnapped some very strange young people and now they're about to rob a bank.

Ken and Jenna looked at each other. "Young people with special gifts?" Ken asked.

Yes, there's one girl who predicts the future and another one who disappears—

"Do you know where they are?" Ken asked.

Of course I know where they are. I'm in heaven. I can see my son whenever I want—

Maybe it wasn't very nice to interrupt the deceased, but this woman could have gone on forever. "Where are they?" Ken and Jenna demanded in unison.

She told them.

CHAPTER THIRTEEN

THERE DIDN'T SEEM TO be anything unusual going on at Northwest National Savings and Loan. From the parking lot, Jenna could make out the shadows of figures inside the bank, not running or moving in any suspicious manner. She couldn't tell if any of them were her classmates. The four of them left Madame's car and started across the street.

Jenna's senses were on high alert, and she knew she'd pick up the thoughts of her classmates as soon as she was close enough. But she didn't expect to hear Emily while she was still in the parking lot.

I wish I could be inside with the rest of them. I can't even see what's going on.

"I hear Emily!" she told the others.

"Is she in the bank?" Madame asked.

"No. The others are inside, and she's thinking

about how she wishes she could be with them. I'm sure she's in one of these cars." But there were at least twenty cars in the parking lot, and she couldn't tell where the thoughts were coming from.

I'm scared. Clare looks so calm and confident, like nothing can possibly go wrong. I'll bet she'd use that gun on me, too, if the others tried to get away. And they might try. They've only got Howard and George in the bank with them, and they're not the sharpest crayons in the box. I don't think they're even armed. Clare's the brains.

"Howard . . . isn't that the name of the dead woman's son?" Jenna asked Ken. "He's in the bank with the others. Emily's in a car with someone called Clare, and Clare's got a gun."

"If I knew which car they were in, I could get the gun away from her," Charles said.

"Okay, you and Madame find the car," Jenna said. "Ken and I will go into the bank."

"No," Madame said. "Wait until we get the gun. I'm not letting my students go into that place when there's someone around here with a firearm."

Jenna took the handles of Charles's wheelchair.

"Maybe Emily's thoughts will get louder when we get closer," she said. She began pushing Charles between two rows of cars.

"Don't go so fast, Jenna," Madame chided her. "You don't want to attract attention. I think this Clare person just might notice someone running with a wheelchair in a parking lot. Not to mention the fact that she might recognize both of you."

"How?" Jenna wanted to know. "She hasn't seen me."

Madame spoke quietly. "You don't know that, Jenna. I have a very strong feeling that this Clare is no ordinary criminal. And this is no ordinary bank robbery."

Jenna had no idea what she was talking about, and she couldn't worry about it now. But she slowed her pace, and Ken and Madame followed closely behind. Jenna kept her eyes and ears open and hoped her special ability was in prime working order.

I wish I could see what was happening in the bank. The guard—he wouldn't shoot a kid, would he? Even if the kid was trying to rob the bank?

Emily's thoughts were definitely louder. Despite Madame's warning, Jenna quickened her pace. Was it that truck over there? Or maybe the green car with the dent in the bumper. If only the lights in the parking lot were brighter so she could see people inside the cars . . .

"It's the SUV," Ken whispered.

Jenna stopped. "How do you know?"

"Howard's mother. She just told me it used to be her car."

Jenna brought the wheelchair up behind the SUV. She bent down to speak into Charles's ear. "Can you sense the gun yet?"

"No. I have to get around to the driver's side. Let go of the chair."

Something told Jenna not to argue. She lifted her hands. Slowly, Charles began pushing himself around to the side of the vehicle. Jenna stayed behind with Madame and Ken. She held her breath, and she couldn't hear any breathing coming from the other two either.

Suddenly the driver's window rolled down. Jenna heard a woman's voice.

"What the—"

And then a gun came flying out of the window. Ken's former life as an athlete came in handy, as he ran and caught it. Then all the car doors opened. Emily leaped out, and at the same time, the car started up. Jenna and Madame leaped out of the way as the SUV backed out. With doors still open, it sped out of the parking lot.

Charles spun his wheelchair around, but it was too late. The big car was out of his sight before he could stop it.

Jenna didn't care. She was too busy hugging Emily tightly. Only for a second though. Jenna wasn't into public displays of affection.

"The others are in the bank," Emily told them.

"We know," Madame said. "Are the men with them armed?"

"I don't think so."

"We're armed," Ken said proudly, holding the gun.

"Put that down," Madame snapped. "I don't want any shooting. I'm calling the police. You stay here."

She took out her cell phone. Jenna looked at Emily with her eyebrows raised.

She told Ken to stay put. Not us.

Jenna nodded. She grabbed Emily's hand, and while Madame's back was to them, they ran to the bank.

CHAPTER FOURTEEN

THERE'S MARTIN, TALKING TO the woman behind the counter," Emily said. "He's supposed to break down the door to the vault." She explained how Martin was supposed to demand money and unleash his superpowers when the teller treated him like a stupid little kid. A customer came out of the bank, leaving the door slightly ajar. Now they could hear Martin's shrill voice.

"But I want some money *now*!"

A man wearing a name tag approached him. "I'm the bank manager. Is there a problem here?"

The teller behind the counter spoke. "I'm trying to explain to this young man that we don't give money away."

The manager chuckled. "I see. Come with me, young man. I'll show you how banks operate."

"I just want some money," Martin whined.

"Yes, of course you do," the man said kindly. "And I'm going to show you how to open a savings account and earn interest."

"I don't want interest, I want money!" Martin screamed.

"Where's Tracey?" Jenna asked Emily.

"Well, if my vision was right, she should be invisible. She's supposed to get the money out of the vault. See the curly haired man? That's Howard. The skinny one by the door is George." She turned to Jenna. "How did you find us?"

"Howard's mother," Jenna said. "Long story, tell you later."

Emily clutched Jenna's arm. "Uh-oh, it's happening now!"

They couldn't hear anything, but they could see, and the expression on Martin's face was something they'd seen before. And then, like a tornado, he tore across the room and crashed through a door.

Emily's heart sank when she saw a security guard draw his gun. Then she saw Amanda-Sarah running for the exit before she slipped on the floor and fell, hard.

"Ohmigod!" Emily shrieked. George was reaching inside his coat. For a gun?

She'd never know. Amanda-Sarah, still sitting on the floor, looked at him. And George froze.

Emily stared at the little scene for a second, thinking, *Wow. Amanda really has got the hang of Sarah's gift.* But something was off. Something about Sarah's eyes looked different . . .

Emily gasped. "It's Sarah!"

"Well, of course it's Sarah," Jenna said. "Who else?"

Obviously, Jenna hadn't bothered to read *her* mind.

"Long story," Emily said. "Tell you later."

Then they both clapped their hands over their ears. Three police cars, sirens wailing and red lights flashing, pulled up in front of the bank. Six officers jumped out of the cars and ran in, shouting for everyone to put their hands in the air.

Now Madame, Ken, and Charles were by their side.

"What happened?" Madame asked in bewilderment. "I hadn't called the police yet."

They heard Tracey's voice before they saw her. "I pushed the alarm button." Now Tracey was visible and beaming happily. "It's silent in the bank, but it alerts the police that something's going on. As I sneaked into the vault, I looked over my shoulder and saw you outside. I knew Emily must be safe, so I ducked back out the vault door and hit the button under the tellers' counter before Martin even broke the door down. How did you get away from Clare, Emily?"

"Charles got the gun," Emily told her.

Tracey stared in disbelief at the boy in the wheelchair. Charles gave her a haughty look. "I'm the real hero," he said.

Emily was sure he'd never let them forget it either. But that was okay with her.

Martin was the next to emerge from the bank. "That teller didn't bother me," he announced. "I used my strength all on my own."

Emily didn't have the heart to tell him they'd heard the whole thing—he'd definitely lost his temper.

Sarah followed him. She was the only one among

them who didn't look relieved or happy. She actually seemed a little bit sad. She slipped past the others and stood beside Madame.

"I had to do it," she whispered.

"I know," Madame said and put a comforting arm around her.

Emily looked at her curiously. Had it been that awful for Sarah, using her gift? Maybe someday she'd learn why the girl was so sad.

Two police officers emerged. One had George in handcuffs, and the other had Howard. As they passed, Ken spoke.

"Howard, your mother is not very happy with you."

Howard gaped at him. George's eyes were searching the parking lot. But Clare was long gone.

Another policeman came out. "Are you all okay?"

"Yes officer, we're fine," Madame said.

He shook his head in puzzlement and looked at Martin. "One of the tellers, she said she saw this boy break open the door to the vault."

Madame let out an odd little artificial laugh. "Well, that's hardly possible, is it, officer?"

He shrugged. "I guess one of the robbers set up an explosive charge and it went off when the kid was by the door. Good thing you weren't hurt, young man."

"Nothing hurts me," Martin bragged. Madame grabbed his arm. "Ow!"

"You didn't get all the bad guys," Emily told the policeman. She explained about Clare. The policeman took out a notebook.

"Can you give me a description of this Clare?"

Emily, Tracey, and Martin exchanged looks. What could they say?

"Blue eyes," they chorused, and then fell silent.

The officer smiled. "Don't worry, kids, I know you're still pretty upset. We'll get details from the guys we caught." He closed his notebook. "So who's the hero here?"

Emily glanced at Sarah.

"Tracey hit the alarm button," Sarah said softly.

"But this is the real hero," Tracey said, putting her hand on Charles's shoulder.

"He got the gun away from Clare," Emily added. Madame glared at her, and she bit her lip.

"Here's the gun, officer," Ken said quickly and handed it over.

"Good work, young man," the policeman said.

Emily looked at Charles. She wasn't surprised to see that he was pouting. She knelt by the wheelchair.

"Don't worry, Charles. We know you're the real hero. And we're going to treat you like one."

Slowly, his face cleared. His cheeks reddened. He *smiled*. And without even trying to look into his future, Emily suspected that it was going to be very different from what she might have predicted for him just days earlier.

Chapter Fifteen

"ARE YOU SURE YOU want to go to school?" Emily's mother asked anxiously on Monday morning. "It seems to me you need more than a weekend to recover."

"I feel fine, Mom," Emily assured her. She got out of the car in front of Meadowbrook. "Don't worry. I'll see you later."

She had to admit, she felt a little tired. But she hadn't wanted to stay at home. More than anything, Emily wanted her life to get back to normal.

She still couldn't believe all the events of the past week. She'd returned home Friday night feeling as if she'd been away for a month. So many emotions . . . she'd been scared, confused, angry, depressed . . . and what was she feeling now?

She wasn't sure. But she knew it wasn't bad. And she knew she'd learned something about herself.

Madame had told them all to come to her room first thing in the morning before school started for a debriefing. Emily was glad she wouldn't have to wait until the gifted class to see everyone. Having been through this adventure, would they be closer as a group?

She wasn't the first one to arrive at room 209. Jenna was already there. She nodded at Emily.

"How do you feel?"

"A little tired," Emily admitted. "But okay. How are you?"

"Okay," Jenna echoed. But Emily thought she looked even more tired than Emily felt. Her eyes were unusually dark.

"I'm glad it's over," Emily said.

"Me, too," Jenna said. And she smiled—but to Emily, it looked a little forced.

Ken came in next, and *he* was definitely in good spirits. "I feel great," he told the girls. "You know, I always felt like I had the most worthless gift. I couldn't do anything with it. Yesterday, for the first time, it paid off!"

"How's that?" Emily asked.

"Jenna read Carter's mind, and that's how we knew about the house. But then this dead woman told me where you were! She was the mother of one of the kidnappers—Howard. She wanted me to give him a message."

"What was the message?" Emily asked.

"She wanted me to tell him he was doing a bad thing and that she was very upset with him. What was he like?"

"He was okay," Emily said. "If I'd met him somewhere else, I might even have thought he was kind of sweet."

Jenna looked surprised. "Your kidnapper was *sweet*?"

"Yeah, that one was. The other man was okay, too. I don't think either of them was very smart, but they were never mean to us. The woman, Clare . . . she was scary."

"She knew how to dress though. I mean, the woman had style." That comment came from Amanda. Back in her own body, she sauntered into the room and took her seat. Then she examined her fingernails. "Whatever takes over my body when I'm out of it does a very nice manicure."

Charles wheeled himself into the room. Emily nudged Ken, and the two of them began applauding.

"Charles, you saved my life," Emily declared. "I wish you could have seen Clare's face when that gun flew out of her hand!"

Charles looked pleased, but a little embarrassed, too. He wasn't used to anyone making a fuss over him.

Tracey arrived next, followed by Martin. Then Carter Street walked in.

Their eyes were on him as he went to his seat and sat down, but, as usual, he didn't react.

"I wonder why they just let him go," Ken mused.

"Because he didn't have a talent they could use, I guess," Tracey suggested.

"Then why did they take him in the first place?" Emily wondered. "They seemed to know everything about all of us."

No one could answer that, and the classmates sat in silence for a moment.

The last student to enter was Sarah. She went directly to Amanda.

"I want to thank you."

Amanda stared at her. "For what?"

"For taking over my body."

Emily was very surprised. "You're glad Amanda snatched your body?"

Sarah nodded. "It put me in a position where I had to use my gift. But I didn't use it before I absolutely needed to. If I'd been in control, I might have been tempted to use it earlier." And she took her seat.

Once again, Emily couldn't help wondering why Sarah was so anxious to avoid using her gift. It was one mystery that definitely hadn't been cleared up.

Finally Madame arrived. "Good morning, class. I won't keep you long, and we can spend more time talking during our regular class time. But while your memory is still fresh, I have to ask you something. What kind of an effect has this experience had on you in regard to your gift? Do you feel different about it now?"

"I do," Ken said. "I actually got something useful from one of my voices."

Charles had something to say, too. "It was kind of

cool, using my gift to save Emily. That lady probably wouldn't have killed her, but—"

"But you never know," Emily said. "Thank you, Charles."

Madame looked at Emily. "What about you, Emily? Have your feelings about your gift changed?"

Emily took a deep breath.

"Yes. Now I know I really have a gift, and it's just as good as everyone else's. Looking back now, everything I've envisioned has come true."

Martin interrupted. "Wait a minute. You said the bank robbery would be a success, and it wasn't."

Emily nodded. "That's because I assumed it would be because I saw Tracey get into the vault and you break the vault door. But I didn't envision the end result—I was just guessing."

"What about the two different visions you had of me?" Amanda wanted to know. "I mean, of me-as-Sarah? First you said I'd have her gift, and then you said I wouldn't have it."

"That's because you fell down," Emily said simply. "And I didn't see that. You wouldn't have been able to freeze George. But you *did* fall, and I guess that's what pushed you out of Sarah's body. Sarah came back into herself and froze George. In my vision, I saw all the possibilities." She grinned. "Maybe the floor was waxed that day and a butterfly flew past the floor cleaner and she left too much wax on one spot."

Madame smiled. "The butterfly effect. I suppose it could have an impact on predictions."

"There's more," Emily said. "I have to learn to separate what I see in my visions from what I want to see. Like, I saw Martin would throw a sofa, and he did. But I'd only hoped he would throw it and break a door down—I didn't see that in the vision. And I have to look for details in the visions. Calendars, watches, newspapers—anything that might indicate a day or a time. I need to notice what people look like. Does someone have a suntan? That could mean the event I'm envisioning is going to happen in the summer." She went on to tell them about the vision she'd had of her mother's bad haircut, and how she thought the vision was a failure because her mother's hair came out okay.

"Looking back, I realize that in the vision, my mother was wearing her heavy quilted coat. The bad haircut will happen in the winter." She smiled. "Anyway, I know I still have to work on my gift. I need to practice examining and interpreting my visions. But at least now I know for sure that I have a gift. And it has value."

"Very good, Emily," Madame said with approval. "Now you can begin to use your gift realistically."

Emily was feeling pretty good when she left the classroom with Tracey. "I'll tell you the best thing that came out of this whole experience," she confided. "My mother's giving me a cell phone. Of course, she'll probably call me every ten minutes on it." She shivered and stopped. "I left my sweater in 209. I'd better go back and get it."

"See you at lunch," Tracey said.

Emily went back to the classroom, but she paused outside the door when she heard voices. She recognized them—Madame and Jenna were talking.

She knew it wasn't right to eavesdrop, but something about the intensity in Jenna's tone kept her there, listening.

"I read her mind, Madame. Clare—before she got away. It was just a glimpse, but I learned something.

She didn't care about robbing that bank. This was a test—of us. Some of us, at least."

"I was afraid of that," Madame said. "What was she testing—the extent of their gifts?"

"Yes, but more than that. She wanted to see how much resistance the students would present—if they could be manipulated and coerced. I can understand why they didn't take me. I'd have read their minds and known what they were really up to. I don't know why they didn't take Charles or Ken. Or Amanda. Well, they did take Amanda, but it was an accident. But this whole thing, it had nothing to do with robbing a bank. It was an experiment, Madame."

"And was she pleased with the results of the experiment?" Madame asked.

Emily had to strain to hear Jenna's low voice. "Yes. And she didn't care what happened to Howard or George. There are other people involved, but not them. And the other people—they've got plans. I don't know what the plans are, Madame, but I think something big is going on. Something a lot bigger than a bank robbery."

Madame spoke calmly. "Yes, I can believe that, Jenna."

"Who *are* these people, Madame? What do they want?"

"I'm not sure. But you're right, Jenna. They're planning something. And they're very dangerous."

"What are we going to do, Madame?"

"We're going to work together, and you're going to learn how to use your gifts defensively."

"Are you worried?"

Emily wished she could see Madame's face. She had a feeling it might tell her more than her words.

"I'm not worried about you, Jenna. Or your classmates. I'm worried for the world. And how my gifted students are going to have to save it."

There was a silence in the classroom. Which was fine with Emily. She didn't want to hear any more. She could leave her sweater there for the time being.

The halls were crowded now as people hurried to their first classes. Emily hurried, too, and tried not to think about the conversation she'd overheard. But she had to think about it because it was there, in her head, and it couldn't be pushed aside. And the questions went around and around.

What did those people want from them? Who were they, really? Would she be called upon to predict their motives? And how could a handful of middle school teenagers save the world? So much to think about, to worry about . . .

But oddly enough, she didn't feel panicked. She and her classmates *were* special. They had gifts. Maybe now they'd begin to learn the real purpose of those gifts. Hearing voices, reading minds, snatching bodies—there was a reason why they had these unique talents. Maybe now, in the face of something really big, they'd learn how to use them in the best possible way.

Emily would have her visions. She'd try to see what she could in the future and try to understand what she was seeing. She'd look for clues and read between the lines. She would interpret; she'd weed out the irrelevancies.

And always keep her eyes open for butterflies.

I

GIFTED

Out of Sight, Out of Mind

ONE MORNING AMANDA LOOKED IN THE MIRROR AND ANOTHER GIRL LOOKED BACK...

Amanda Beeson is Queen Bee at Meadowbrook school. If you're not friends with Amanda, you're nobody. But one morning gorgeous, popular Amanda Beeson looks in the mirror and sees a very different face staring back at her. The Queen Bee is about to get a taste of life in someone else's shoes.

2

GIFTED

BETTER LATE THAN NEVER

IF JENNA CAN'T TRUST HER DAD, WHO CAN SHE TURN TO?

Tough rebel Jenna Kelley secretly dreams of a conventional life with normal parents. When her mother ends up in rehab, Jenna is shocked by the sudden reappearance of her long-lost dad. Jenna can usually read anyone's mind, but this stranger is a total mystery. Before long, streetwise Jenna finds herself walking straight into danger.

3

GIFTED

FiNDERS
KEEPERS

YOUR PROBLEMS DON'T GO AWAY
JUST BECAUSE YOU'RE DEAD.

Dead people don't make great companions. Cute, athletic Ken finds that out the hard way when, following an accident on the soccer field, he starts hearing ghostly voices. It's not a gift he would have asked for—especially when it gets him involved in a love triangle with his dead best friend's girlfriend—but there's nothing he can do about it . . . until an anonymous note invites him to a séance. Completely convinced by the medium he meets, Ken tries to tell her about his secret. Only his gifted classmates can save him from revealing the truth—and finding himself in terrible peril . . .

Publishing in April 2010